Hollywood Malice

Roman St. John

Hollywood Malice

I dedicate this book to
my amazing friends

Hollywood Malice

Chapter 1

John Parker's cell phone was ringing, but he wasn't going to answer it. Why should he? He knew exactly who it was. It was his tormenter, and right now he really wasn't in the mood to be tormented.

John shuddered every time he saw the words 'private call' flash across his phone. Who could the caller be, and what exactly was it that he wanted? Why had he called almost everyday for the past two weeks?

His cell phone stopped ringing.

Trying to block out his problems, John continued to work on his screenplay. He had only been writing for an hour this morning and the last thing he needed right now was a distraction. If he didn't finish the script soon, he was going to be ruined. He had no income coming in, and his savings were quickly drying up.

His cell phone began ringing again. He looked at the phone and saw that it was him again, the tormenter. The man never gave up.

John's face was fiery red with rage. He decided that it was high time he put an end to this little game once and for all.

"What do you want from me?" he exploded into the phone. "I'm sick of your demented games!"

The mysterious caller just laughed.

"Patience, my friend," he said, his voice sounding evil. "You must have patience. And please don't be so rude. I find it highly offensive."

The nerve of this guy! Who did he think he was?

"I don't care what you find offensive," John ranted. "I find it offensive that you continue to call me after I've told you that I don't want to talk to you unless you tell me who you are."

"Revealing my identity to you is out of the question, John."

"Then don't call me again. This is your last warning. If you don't heed my advice and leave me alone, then I'm going to file a police report and find out exactly who you are."

"I wouldn't do that if I were you," the voice warned. "You'll only be hurting yourself if you do."

John wasn't buying it.

"Oh yeah," he challenged. "How is that? What are *you* going to do about it?"

The caller didn't respond.

"Answer me," John yelled. "How will I be hurting myself?"

"I could ruin you, John," the voice said. "I know things about you…things you don't want anyone to know…things from your past… secrets from your past." He paused. "I know about your precious Kelly and the girls."

John's throat went dry. How was this possible? How could anyone have found out? He thought he had covered his tracks so well.

"I don't know what you're talking about," he lied, trembling with fear. What else could he say? He wasn't about to admit anything. Not after all these years.

"Don't play games with me," the caller said. "I know exactly who you are, and you know exactly what I'm talking about. You keep no secrets from me. I know everything about you, John. In fact, I want to be you. I want your car, I want your house. I even want your girlfriend."

"Please just tell me why you keep calling me?" John said, giving up on the attitude. It wasn't doing him any good. This caller had power over him, and there wasn't a thing he could do about it.

"I want to possess you," the voice said. "I want to become one with John Parker."

Chapter 2

"How are the two classiest women in LA doing today?" a smiling, tanned-faced Vincent said to Elizabeth Herrington and her friend Kim Whiteside. The two women, both attractive and in their late thirties, were enjoying a late lunch on the patio at Donatello's, one of the most popular eating spots in Los Angeles. The restaurant was always the place to be among Hollywood's elite, and today was no different. Elizabeth and Kim had already spotted several celebrities.

"We're doing great, Vincent," Elizabeth answered, returning his smile. "How's our favorite waiter doing?"

Vincent, an energetic and athletic-looking guy of twenty-three, had been working as a waiter there for years.

"Fabulous! We've been staying busy today. This place has been packed for the last three hours." He gave Kim a wink. He was totally in love with her, and had been for the last several years, despite the fact that he usually only dated men.

"Your husband was here earlier, Kim" he said.

"Ex-husband!" she snapped. "You know that, Vincent!"

He laughed heartily.

"I can't resist messing with your head."

"Screw you," she joked, lightening up. "Was he with that blonde again?" She couldn't keep herself from asking.

"No, this time he was with a brunette."

"Hmph," Kim snorted. "It's a new one every week with him."

"Aren't *we* the bitter one?" Elizabeth suddenly chimed in, giving Vincent a sly smile.

"I know," he echoed her. "I think someone's *jealous*."

"Don't you have work to do, Vincent?" Kim sighed, pretending to be exasperated.

"As a matter of fact, I do," he said, and with that he hurried off. "So, how's Peter?" Kim asked when Vincent was gone, wanting to change the subject.

Elizabeth had recently married Dr. Peter Herrington, a sixty-two-year-old prominent Beverly Hills plastic surgeon.

"Good, I guess," Elizabeth sighed, staring off into space.

"What do you mean, you guess? Tell me there's not trouble in paradise already?"

"No, Peter and I are perfectly happy. It's Allison who has the problem."

Kim, who had just finished her own meal, was now picking away at Elizabeth's.

"Tell me more," she said. "This sounds juicy."

"Allison's still not happy about the marriage at all. I don't think she's ever going to fully accept it."

Allison was Peter's nineteen-year-old-daughter from his first marriage, and was the best friend of Elizabeth's own daughter, Cameron, who was also nineteen. The two of them had been best friends since elementary school and were now stepsisters."

"Allison will get over it," Kim said. "You two will be the best of friends in no time."

"Oh, Allison doesn't have anything against me. We get along great. She's just irritated with her dad for marrying someone so much younger than him."

"Why don't you get Cameron to talk to her?"

"I think I will," Elizabeth decided. She'd talk to her daughter about it tonight. Cameron and Allison were on a shopping spree at The Grove right now.

"How is Steven handling everything?" Kim asked. Steven was Peter's son.

"Oh, he's fine with the marriage," Elizabeth said. "*If you know what I mean.*"

Kim gave her a knowing look.

"Oh, I know what you mean," she said, rolling her eyes. "Has the little playboy tried to make a move on you yet?"

"Only all the time."

"Does he still live at home?"

"No, he lives at our beach house in Malibu, but he stops by several times a week. He's nothing but a bum who's going nowhere in life. He doesn't have any goals. He's not in school and doesn't even have a job."

"What does he do all day?"

"I think he drinks a lot. Staying drunk keeps him occupied."

"I'm surprised his mother doesn't put a stop to that," Kim said, referring to Peter's ex-wife, Harmon Herrington, who was a former child television star. "She doesn't seem like the type that would just let him sit around and waste his life like that."

"Harmon doesn't care. She's too into herself to have time to worry about Steven."

"Speaking of Harmon, there she is right there," Kim said, nodding towards a nearby table. Elizabeth turned to look. In her early fifties, Harmon Herrington was a strikingly attractive woman. Tall and slender with jet black hair, the woman was a socialite in every sense of the word. She was one of the biggest snobs in Beverly Hills. She never missed a party and she only associated with LA's most affluent… the super-rich and celebrities. She snubbed almost everyone else she came in contact with, and virtually no one who knew her blamed Peter for getting rid of her.

Harmon's eyes met Elizabeth's. Elizabeth smiled and gave her a friendly wave. Harmon managed to return the wave with a slight raise of her hand. It was always a strain for her to acknowledge people who she felt were beneath her on the Beverly Hills social ladder. It didn't help that Elizabeth was now married to her ex.

"Who's that guy she's with?" Kim asked.

"That's her boyfriend, John Parker," Elizabeth said, waving to him too. "He's nothing like her. I met him at a party at the Bel-Air Country Club a couple of weeks ago. He's very nice."

"I wonder why he puts up with *her*?"

Elizabeth shrugged her shoulders. "She's very attractive. I guess maybe that's why."

Kim was still checking Harmon and John out. "He looks a good bit younger than her," she said.

"Yeah, I think he's in his late thirties…closer to our age."

"I hope he's just using her for her money," Kim said, not trying to hide her disdain for Harmon.

Even though Kim was a millionaire herself, Harmon had always thought she was better than her, and it had always kind of made her mad. She knew that the only reason she snubbed her was because she wasn't a member of the super-rich like herself.

Harmon had grown up in Beverly Hills and had been groomed by her parents to be a huge star. As a young child, she landed several leading roles in hit television shows and even did a couple of award winning movies. Her acting career had worked out while she was still a kid, but as she got older and entered her teen years, she quit getting parts and eventually gave up show business altogether. After her acting career fizzled, her new goal became making sure she married rich, which she succeeded in doing when she married Peter.

"I don't know why she still thinks she's so high and mighty," Kim scorned. "You're not married to Peter Herrington anymore, little Miss Harmon," she said, looking towards Harmon. "Elizabeth is, though."

Elizabeth couldn't help but laugh.

"Kim, you crack me up," she said, motioning Vincent over to their table. "We're ready for our check," she said.

Chapter 3

John Parker was sick and tired of his girlfriend, Harmon Herrington. She was nothing but a miserable, controlling nag. He wished that he had never moved in with her.

When is she ever going to shut up? he wondered, finally giving up on watching TV. She had been complaining about her ex-husband, Peter, and his new wife, Elizabeth, for almost an hour and a half now.

"Elizabeth just has no class," Harmon said once again. "She doesn't know how to behave properly in social situations."

John didn't tell her that he begged to differ. In his opinion, Elizabeth was one of the classiest women he had ever met. He would give anything to date a woman like her.

"I just don't understand why Peter married her," Harmon continued. "I'll never understand it."

There were definitely some things that John didn't understand either, one being how he had become stuck with Harmon Herrington. Sure, she was attractive, but she was so incredibly hard to get along with. She was the most spoiled person he'd ever met. She valued money and material things more than anything else. John knew that he was never going to be able to provide for her the way her wealthy parents and Peter Herrington had. He was a screenwriter, and a very poor one at that. Unfortunately for him, he had so far had no luck selling his scripts. Even though he dreamed of his luck one day changing, right now he had no source of income. He lived off the small inheritance his parents had left him when they died in a house fire ten years earlier. This sum of money was in no way enough to support Harmon's extravagant lifestyle.

All John wanted to do at this point was to get out of this miserable relationship and he planned on doing just that as soon as he found a place of his own. He had been looking at nearby townhouses all week. He was keeping this a secret from Harmon, though. There was no telling what she would do if she found out he was going to leave her.

Harmon knew that something was up, though. She could tell just by looking at John. All she knew was that he had better not be planning on leaving her. She had already decided what she was going to do to him if he did leave her, though. She would have him killed just like she was going to have Peter killed for divorcing her. No one messed with Harmon Herrington and got away with it.

Chapter 4

Having just taken a shower after lying out by the pool for a while at her gorgeous Beverly Hills mansion, Elizabeth Herrington was attempting to clean her bedroom when her cell phone rang.

"Hello," she answered. It was her daughter, Cameron.

"What's up Mom?" Cameron asked enthusiastically.

"Oh, nothing much," Elizabeth replied. "I haven't done anything too terribly exciting. Kim and I got together earlier. We met for lunch at Donatello's. She's leaving tomorrow for England. Her sister lives in London and wanted her to go visit for a couple of months, so it was good that we got to spend some quality time together before she leaves."

"Sounds fun," Cameron said.

"So what have you been up to today?" Elizabeth asked. "Are you and Allison still shopping?"

"Yeah, I'm on the way home now. Allison's meeting up with her mother to shop a little longer, though."

"That's good," Elizabeth responded. "We're eating at Mastro's Steakhouse tonight. Wanna come?"

"Who else is going to be there?" Cameron asked cautiously. She didn't want to be around Steven, Peter's son. He always hit on her and she wasn't comfortable with it, especially now that he was her stepbrother.

"It's going to be me, Peter, Allison, and hopefully you."

"I take it Steven's not going then."

"I wouldn't be going if he was," Elizabeth said. "I'm definitely not in the mood for him today."

Cameron chuckled. "You're such a loving stepmother, Mom," she kidded.

"Hey, I do my best. Oh, guess what?" Elizabeth suddenly exclaimed excitedly, remembering that she had forgotten to tell Cameron that she had seen Harmon at lunch. "You'll never guess who Kim and I saw at Donatello's?"

"Steven," Cameron sighed.

"No, guess again."

"I have no idea."

"Harmon."

"Did you go up to her and start a conversation?" Cameron joked. She was well aware of the fact that Peter's ex-wife couldn't stand Elizabeth.

"Yeah right," Elizabeth said. "I value my life." She paused. "I don't know why she hates me so much," she continued. "I'm so good to her kids. Allison and I are becoming really close."

"The reason she hates you so much is because she's jealous of you. You're young and full of life. She's not. That intimidates her. Besides, she wants Peter back so bad she can taste it."

"No she doesn't," Elizabeth said naively. "She's dating that John Parker guy. They're living together now."

"But John Parker's not rich, and a rich man is what women like Harmon want."

Deep down, Elizabeth knew her daughter was right. Harmon was never going to be happy with John. She didn't want to gossip about it, though. In a way, she almost felt sorry for Harmon because she was such an unhappy woman."

"So are you going to meet us at Mastro's Steakhouse tonight?" she asked again, changing the subject.

"Count me in," Cameron said.

Elizabeth suddenly decided to go ahead and let her daughter in on the news.

"Hey Cameron," she whispered excitedly into the phone. "If I tell you something, can I trust you to keep it a secret for the next few hours?"

"Yeah, you know you can trust me."

"You can't even tell Allison," Elizabeth said. "If you do, it'll spoil the whole surprise."

"What surprise?" Cameron asked impatiently. "What are you talking about? What's going on?"

"I'm pregnant," Elizabeth whispered. "Peter and I are going to have a baby."

"Pregnant!" Cameron exclaimed, completely thrilled. "Oh Mom, that's great."

"Now remember you can't tell anyone," Elizabeth warned. "I haven't even told Peter yet. I'm going to announce it to the family tonight at dinner. I couldn't wait any longer to tell you, though. I had to tell someone. I was about to burst with the news."

"How far along are you?" Cameron asked.

"About six weeks," she gushed. "I've got to go," she suddenly whispered hurriedly. "One of the maids is knocking at my bedroom door. I'll see you in a few minutes when you get home."

"See you in a few," Cameron said, still beaming. She was so excited for her mother.

Chapter 5

"I can't believe it's the week!" Allison Herrington squealed to her best friend Cameron. "It's the week of my debut in *Deceptive Intentions*…the week I become a big star. Can you believe it?"

The two drop dead gorgeous blondes were sitting out on the terrace at the Herrington mansion, relaxing after spending an exhausting day of shopping all over LA. Allison had shopped even longer than Cameron because she'd met up with her mother later in the afternoon.

"What makes you so certain that you're going to become a big star?" Cameron laughed, always amazed by how much confidence her stepsister had.

"Oh, come on," Allison replied, the tone of her voice incredulous. "You know I will! I've worked really hard for this. When the world sees me on the screen, they'll fall in love with me."

"I sure hope you're right," Cameron said.

"Me too," Allison giggled, displaying doubt for the first time. She wasn't nearly as confident about it as she made herself out to be. In actuality, she was very nervous about the whole thing. "My mom will kill me if I don't make it big this time. She keeps telling me that this is my huge chance."

"How *is* your mom?" Cameron asked. "I haven't seen her in a while." Despite the fact that Harmon Herrington was a snob and extremely hard to get along with, there was something about her that impressed Cameron. She wasn't quite sure what it was, but she thought it might be the way she carried herself—with extreme confidence, just like her daughter.

"She's fine, I guess," Allison said vaguely. "Same as always. She's never been much of a mother, you know. She's too into herself. It's really kind of sad when you think about it. We did have fun shopping this afternoon, though."

Cameron was well aware of the fact that Harmon would absolutely flip out if Allison didn't become the next big Hollywood star. It would absolutely devastate her. Even though she didn't spend much time with her kids, Harmon still wanted them to be the center of attention. By pushing her daughter to become famous, she was advancing her own social situation.

"You're lucky to have such a cool mom," Allison said, referring to Elizabeth. She reached for her cell phone which was ringing.

"Hello," she answered. It was Carter Greenfield, her boyfriend of two and a half months now.

"Hey sexy," he said in his deep voice.

"What's up baby?" Allison giggled in her most flirtatious voice. Cameron rolled her eyes and made a gagging sound.

"You two disgust me," she murmured.

"Not much," Carter said. "Just been hanging out at the beach here in Malibu all day…did some surfing"

"Well, do you want to drive down and eat dinner with us tonight at Mastro's Steakhouse?" she asked him.

"Who's us?"

"My family."

"Sure, sounds good. What time?"

"Elizabeth said seven o'clock. Does that work for you?"

"Sure does," Carter said. "I'll be there by seven." Allison knew fully well that he would be. Unlike her, he was never late.

"See you then, and I love you," she drooled.

Cameron rolled her eyes again.

"I love you more," he said. They both clicked off.

"You two need to get over yourselves," Cameron laughed, making fun of her stepsister. "I love you, baby," she mocked. "You're the best thing that's ever happened to me."

"Shut up!" Allison snapped jokingly, lighting up a cigarette. "At least I *have* a boyfriend."

"Hey, I'm single and proud of it," Cameron retorted playfully. "You're not supposed to be smoking, you know," she added. "Remember the pact we made—no more smoking."

"Yeah, yeah," Allison sighed, blowing the smoke out of her mouth. "I'll quit tomorrow. One more day of rebellion won't hurt."

Cameron laughed.

"You know," she said, changing the subject. "I still can't believe my mom married your dad. That's crazy that we've been friends all these years and now we're family."

"I guess," Allison said, shrugging her shoulders. "You know how things are here in Hollywood. It's not nearly as big as everyone thinks it is. Everyone knows everyone." She paused and giggled. "Everyone sleeps with everyone."

Cameron only laughed at Allison and shook her head.

As Allison looked at her stepsister, she felt a little guilty for not telling her what was going on with her. She and Cameron usually told each other everything, but this time was different. Most likely she was about to become famous and she wasn't about to ruin her big week, even if keeping a secret this large caused her to feel guilty. She was going to wait a while before she told Cameron or anyone else the truth—that she was pregnant, and with Carter's baby.

Chapter 6

Dr. Peter Herrington, plastic surgeon to the stars, was speeding in his Porsche down Sunset Boulevard towards Mastro's Steakhouse to meet his family for dinner. It had been a long day at the hospital, and he was very tired. Mondays were always a bitch.

He glanced at his watch. Five minutes till seven. He was going to be a few minutes late, but that was okay. When his wife, Elizabeth, had told him to be there by seven, she was undoubtedly aware not to expect him until at least ten after. He was never on time, and everyone he knew was used to it by now. Thankfully the traffic was light or he would be even later.

"Damnit!" he yelled, closing his eyes and taking a deep breath as he slammed on his brakes as the traffic light he was quickly approaching turned red. Everything was getting to him lately. He was a nervous wreck, and it was no wonder. He was sixty-two years-old and nothing ever went his way. Everything about his train wreck of a life was depressing.

The light turned green and he quickly pressed the accelerator to the floor. He prayed that he wouldn't get a speeding ticket.

Peter had spent a lot of time lately trying to figure out how he had screwed up his life so much. How had he allowed the woman he wanted to be with to slip through his fingers? He was thinking of Harmon, his faithful girlfriend through medical school…the mother of his two kids…his ex-wife.

"My ex-wife," Peter lamented allowed. "How did this happen to us, Harmon? How did this happen?"

He knew good and well how it had happened, though. He had thought that he could just trade her in for a newer model…a younger and sexier one. And why shouldn't he have thought that? That's what all the other doctors at the hospital did, and they seemed to be happy. As soon as their wives hit forty, those guys were bringing out the divorce papers…signing on the dotted line…twenty or more years of marriage down the drain with the stroke of a pen. Peter had only been following the trend. Some good it had done him. Now he was stuck with Elizabeth, the newer model, some thirty-something-year-old he could give a flip about. Not that Elizabeth wasn't nice and attractive. She was both of those things, but she just wasn't his type. He had given up his life with Harmon for…a constant state of misery.

Peter knew that he didn't have a chance of winning Harmon back now. She was happily involved with that joke of a guy who called himself a screenwriter. John Parker, his name was…in Peter's opinion, a real jackass. Apparently, the two of them thought they were little geniuses because according to the private investigator that Peter had hired to track Harmon's every move, they were cooking up a plan equal with none other, or at least Harmon was. The investigator still wasn't quite sure what it was yet, but whatever it was, it involved a shady guy named Leonard Holt, who was rumored to be a professional hit man. Yeah, that's right. A hit man…of all things. Harmon had had lunch with the sleaze bag three times over the past two weeks. They were obviously in the process of negotiating. It looked like someone was going to be killed and Peter had a good idea Harmon meant for it to be him. Who else would she want dead? As far as he knew, he was the only person she regarded as a real enemy. She had been furious with him ever since the divorce was finalized.

The most bizarre thing about this whole hit man thing was that Harmon would in no way financially benefit from his death. All the money she would ever get from him, she had received in a lump sum in the divorce settlement. Money was definitely not her motive. Her motive was simpler than that. She wanted revenge…she wanted revenge on him for leaving her and embarrassing her in front of everyone she knew. Well, if there was one thing Peter Herrington was sure of, it was that Harmon wasn't going to get her revenge. He would never give her that satisfaction. Not that he didn't want to die, he did. He didn't care anything about living anymore. What was the point? He was sick and tired of being tormented in this endless maze of pain and suffering called life, which was exactly why he was going to commit suicide tonight after eating his last meal at Mastro's Steakhouse. He was going to end his life before Harmon's hit man got the chance to end it for him. For once in his life, Peter was going to be the one in control. He was going to be the one to pull the trigger and there wasn't a damn thing anyone else could do about it.

Chapter 7

Twenty-one-year-old Steven Herrington was living his life exactly the way he wanted, and why the hell shouldn't he? He was rich, young, *and* single. The way he looked at it, partying was his right. Drugs, booze, and wild, wild women. He loved it all. Tonight was Monday night and he had two goals for the evening. The first was to get drunk, and the second was to get laid. The best place to accomplish both of these goals was at Joey's Bar, a topless bar in the Valley, so Joey's was exactly where he was headed.

Steven only had two more miles to go. He was driving the red Mercedes convertible his father, Dr. Peter Herrington, had given him for his high school graduation present three years ago. Receiving such a nice present was supposed to have served as an incentive for him to honor his parents' wishes and enroll in a college somewhere. Honor his parents' wishes? Enroll in a college? Yeah right. Like he would ever have really done something like that. Who needed a college education anyway? What a waste of four years.

Steven had bigger plans than college. He was going to open his own bar one day…a bar just like Joey's. It would be the biggest thing that ever hit LA. With all of the many nights he had spent in bars, he, if anyone should, should know how to run one.

Good drink and even better women. That would be his motto.

He sped into the parking lot of Joey's and brought the flashy convertible to a screeching halt. He was showing out because there were three hot-looking blondes standing by the car parked next to his.

As he got out his convertible, he gave them a wink, and wondered if one of them was going to be the lucky one that got to go home with him tonight.

"Nice wheels," one of the babes remarked, her throaty voice a complete turn-on.

"I make it look good, don't I," he said, flipping his dark brown hair out of his eyes as he kept walking towards the door of the bar. He didn't want to appear too interested. He knew that playing hard to get would drive them wild. Along with his good looks, of course.

All three girls giggled.

"Someone's a little sure of himself," the same blonde was bold enough to kid. Steven only smiled. He had them hooked, and it was only a matter of time until they came inside to talk to him. Girls were attracted to his cockiness.

Inside the bar, he nodded to all of the other regular Monday night drunks…all of whom were divorced men in their mid-forties. None of the younger crowd came during the week. They all partied there on the weekends. Friday and Saturday nights at Joey's were always over the top. Anything and everything happened.

"How's it going?" Joey Bennett, the owner of the place, called out to Steven from behind the bar where he was preparing himself a Jack Daniel's on the rocks. A raging alcoholic, Joey was a grossly overweight man in his early fifties. His wrinkled face was proof of his rough life, which consisted of five failed marriages and years of financial problems.

"Pretty good," Steven said, walking over to him. "Pretty damn good." He paused, looking around to see if he saw Amber, his favorite stripper. His eyes lit up when he spotted her dancing with a pole across the room. Maybe *she* was going to be the lucky one to go home with him tonight.

"Make me one of those," Steven said, nodding at the Jack. He sat down on one of the barstools. "Amber's looking mighty fine tonight," he said. "You sure have good people working for you, Joey."

Joey laughed.

"I need to set you two up," he said. "You'd be perfect together."

Steven raised his eyebrows. It wasn't everyday that someone mentioned setting him up with a stripper.

"Why do you say that?" he asked.

"Oh, she's always talking about you," Joey said as he placed Steven's drink in front of him. "She says she thinks you're a total hunk."

Steven's already super-sized ego was getting bigger by the second. Maybe Amber *was* going to be the lucky one tonight.

Before he could ask anymore questions, the three blondes from the parking lot walked into the bar. They were tripping all over themselves to get a piece of him.

"There he is," Steven heard one of them say. "Over there, talking to Joey."

"Do you know who those girls are?" Steven whispered, lighting up a cigarette. "I haven't seen them around here before."

Joey laughed again.

"Always thinking about women, aren't you, Steven?" he said. "I can't blame you, though. I was the same way when I was your age. Nothing's more exciting than a pretty girl."

Steven took a drag on his cigarette.

"What can I say?" he said, a mischievous grin spreading across his face. "Chasing women is my hobby." He paused. "You never answered my question, though. Do you know who they are?"

"Newcomers," Joey said, poring himself another drink. "The taller one's Samantha something or another. I can't remember her last name. I met her when she came in here the other night, though."

"Taylor," a flirty voice said. It was the same throaty voice that had spoken to him out in the parking lot. "Samantha Taylor."

Steven and Joey both jumped with surprise. They hadn't realized she was standing right beside them. Her two friends were now sitting at a table by the door.

"Can I get a beer?" she said to Joey, perching herself on the barstool next to Steven. "Whatever kind you have," she added. "It doesn't matter what."

Steven had regained his composure from being caught off guard.

"You're an easy to please kind of girl," he said offhandedly, blowing smoke up in the air. "That's exactly what I've been looking for, an easy to please kind of girl."

"Maybe you just found her," Samantha said, lighting a cigarette of her own.

Steven shrugged his shoulders. "Maybe."

His cell phone rang.

"Hello," he answered, ignoring Samantha's looks of adoration at him. It was Carter Greenfield. Carter was his best friend, and his sister Allison's boyfriend. He lived with him at the beach house in Malibu. Rent free, of course.

"Where are you, man?" Carter yelled into the phone. It was only eight o'clock, but he already sounded completely wasted.

"I'm at Joey's," Steven said, putting his cigarette in the ash tray.

"Is Amber there tonight?" Amber was Carter's favorite stripper also.

"Yeah man. You better get over here."

"I'm on my way." Carter clicked off.

"Sorry about that," Steven said, turning to face Samantha. She wasn't there, though. He turned in every direction. She wasn't even in the bar anymore. Neither were her two friends.

"Damnit!" he exploded, banging his fist on the counter. "Where the fuck did she go?"

Joey was smiling at him and shaking his head.

"You blew it man," he said. "Completely and totally blew it. You were acting like you didn't even like her at all."

Steven didn't understand it. He didn't understand it at all. No female ever rejected him. What was wrong with that girl? He was Steven Herrington, the coolest guy around. Couldn't she tell that just by looking at him?

Joey was still shaking his head.

"I can't believe you blew it," he said again.

Not wanting Joey to know that his ego had taken a slam, Steven shrugged his shoulders and pretended not to care anymore.

"It's her loss," he said. "I'm a lot better looking than she is. She'd be lucky to get a guy like me."

Joey only smiled. He wasn't in the mood to argue.

Steven stayed just a little longer. He left a few minutes before nine, not even caring if Carter got mad at him for leaving before he got there. This Samantha girl had ruined his night. He wasn't used to people not kissing up to him and doing everything he wanted them to do.

As he drove away in his Mercedes, Steven assured himself that he would come back tomorrow night and see if Samantha was there. If she was, he was going to buy her a drink. He'd win her over eventually. That he was certain of.

Chapter 8

John Parker had been working on his screenplay all morning and desperately needed a break. Since it was only twelve-thirty and he didn't have to be at the premiere until that night, he decided he'd drive to Starbucks, which was less than ten minutes away from Harmon's house. Sometimes just getting out of the house and being around people gave him inspiration for his writing.

Grabbing the keys to the brand new BMW that Harmon had bought him, John made his way outside the house. As he drove through the streets of Beverly Hills, he started to think about Harmon. She hadn't been home for the last several hours. She was out getting her hair and nails done in anticipation of the premiere today. Her daughter had made her very proud, and she wanted to look her best for the big event.

John was very fond of Allison and was looking forward to seeing her onscreen performance tonight. It seemed weird to him that he absolutely couldn't stand the woman he was dating, but cared a lot about her daughter. Steven, the oldest and most rebellious Herrington offspring, was an entirely different story, however. John had tried to develop a relationship with the boy, but so far had failed miserably. Steven had no intentions of ever getting to know him. This bothered

John, even though he knew it shouldn't. It wasn't his fault that Steven was even more hateful and spiteful than Harmon was.

John was so tired that he could hardly keep his eyes open. He had been awake almost all night making decisions about his future. He felt good about the decisions he had made, and hoped he wouldn't live to regret them. One of his main decisions concerned his writing career. He was only going to continue focusing on writing for another year or so. If he didn't sell his script by then, so be it.

One of his other decisions concerned his future with Harmon. For a while he had been thinking about leaving her. Now he knew for sure that he was going to do it. He wanted to find someone he could spend the rest of his life with. He didn't want to waste anymore time with a woman he despised. A life without a loving wife was the last thing he wanted. He didn't think he could mentally handle it, especially after everything that happened to him back in Atlanta. No one in LA knew about all that. No one here knew about his old life, no one except the mysterious caller who was torturing him.

Six years ago, John Parker had been living a nice life in Atlanta. Only he hadn't been John Parker back then. In those days, he was still able to use his real name, Neil Hudson. Neil had been one of the luckiest guys in town. He'd had a gorgeous wife named Kelly, two beautiful daughters, Molly and Grace, and a great job working as an accountant at a very popular firm. His moderately large salary had only been a fraction of his wife's annual earnings, though. Kelly had been what one would call a moneymaking machine. Her thriving career as a very successful real estate agent had allowed them to taste the finer things in life. The couple had been able to afford almost anything they wanted, including four luxury cars and a sprawling mansion in the trendy Buckhead area of the city. Life had been good, but unfortunately all of that changed one tragic night in late August six years ago. On that terrible night, an intruder had entered his family's home and brutally murdered Kelly and his two daughters. Neil had been in Nashville at the time visiting his aunt, who was dying of cancer. The murders were believed to have happened at approximately three in the morning, four hours after he had left the Nashville hospital where his aunt was a patient and drove to her house in Brentwood less than two miles away from the hospital. It was there that he had spent the night.

Because he had spent the night in his aunt's house alone and there wasn't a witness to back this up, the police didn't believe his story. They reasoned that he could easily have made the drive from Nashville to Atlanta, killed his family, and then driven back to Nashville, where he had been by his aunt's side when she died at nine o'clock the next morning. After six agonizing months of investigation, Neil had been arrested and charged with triple homicide. The police had actually thought that he was capable of murdering his own beloved family, the people who meant more to him than the entire world. His trial lasted for more than five months and was an O.J.-style national media circus, but in the end he was acquitted. The jury didn't think there was enough evidence to convict him and later claimed that they were disturbed by Neil's seeming lack of motive and no prior history of violence.

Two months after the trial ended, Neil sold the Buckhead mansion to help pay legal fees and flew to Chicago, where he underwent massive plastic surgery to completely change his appearance so that he wouldn't constantly be recognized by the media. Following the surgery, he legally changed his name to John Parker and then moved to California. Neil Hudson was left behind for good. He, in essence, had died with his family.

John knew that he shouldn't be reflecting on his past like he was. The memories of his wife and daughters brought back a lot of guilt. He felt guilty for not ever trying to find their real killer. To do so, though, would have taken too much out of him. There was only so much he could handle. It was easier to just forget the past and become a new person, which is what he had chosen to do. Right or wrong, it had been his choice.

John thought about the mysterious phone caller again. Someone knew who he was, and he was going to have to find out who that person was and deal with him. One way or the other, he was going to have to find the guy.

He was now at Starbucks. As he entered the crowded coffee shop, John made the decision not to dwell on any more negative thoughts today. He was determined to have a good day, despite all of the problems he was going through.

Chapter 9

It was two o'clock in the afternoon and Peter Herrington was speeding down Wilshire Boulevard towards his house in Beverly Hills. He'd left the hospital early today, having cancelled his last few appointments. It was Friday afternoon and he was pissed off at the whole world. He'd been forced to endure yet another week of life. His plan of shooting himself Monday night after enjoying a nice family meal at Mastro's Steakhouse had been thwarted by his wife's surprise announcement. It was the surprise from hell. Elizabeth was pregnant. Yeah, that's right, pregnant. Knocked-up. The whole works. What the hell was he supposed to do now? Was this supposed to give him a reason to want to live? Was this supposed to inspire him to run out and join the church choir and embrace life? If so, it wasn't working. He was in no way looking forward to staying around pretending to be Mr. Perfect so that he could raise yet another ungrateful little monster. That's what they all were these days, little monsters. Pocket book drainers. But pretend to be Mr. Perfect was exactly what he was going to do. He was going to face his responsibility to both Elizabeth and the kid, as hard as that was going to be.

Every time Peter had thought about Elizabeth this week, he'd felt guilty. This was so unfair to her. She deserved a husband who actually loved her, not one who was just going through the motions. Now she would probably never get that. She was pregnant by a man who could never give her that.

Peter's cell phone rang.

"Hello," he answered as he swerved to avoid hitting a dog that had just run out in front of him.

"Hey Daddy," an excited voice said. It was his daughter, Allison.

"What's up?" he said, trying to sound as enthusiastic as she did.

"Tonight's the big night," she exclaimed. "I'm so excited. All of my hard work is finally paying off."

"That's great, Allison," he said, genuinely proud. "I wish I could have been there for the private screening last week at your mother's house. You know how busy I've been, though."

What a bunch of bull he was feeding her. He was never too busy to take off work. The only reason he hadn't gone to the screening was because he knew how much his absence would infuriate Harmon. He knew she must be considering having her daughter in a movie to be the crowing achievement of her life thus far. His seeming lack of interest was certain to send her completely over the edge, which was exactly what she deserved. Any woman who hires a hit man to kill her ex-husband deserved to be sent over the edge.

"It's okay, Daddy," Allison said, totally oblivious to her father's spiteful intentions. "I know you'll be there tonight at the get-together before the premiere."

"Get together?" Peter asked with surprise, groaning to himself. What was this about? Nobody had told him anything about a get-together.

"Yes Dad," Allison giggled, her spoiled voice beginning to make him cringe. "Don't be silly. Mom said she called you last week and told you that she was having a small party for me before the premiere. It's only going to be family and close friends."

"I haven't even talked to your mother in over a month," Peter said, fury building in his voice. "She didn't call me and tell me anything. She never lets me know what's going on."

"Oh, it's okay," Allison said, too elated at her success to notice her father's anger. "She must have just forgotten. She's been really busy lately."

Yeah, Peter thought. *Busy hiring a hit man to knock my ass off.*

He would have said more, but he didn't have the heart to ruin his daughter's big day. Besides, what did Harmon matter anyway? She was going to be dead soon after all. Now that he knew Elizabeth was pregnant and that suicide was no longer an option for him, he had decided to hire a hit man to kill Harmon so that she wouldn't be around hiring people to kill him. Peter knew his life was getting complicated, but there wasn't anything he could do about it.

"What time do I need to be there tonight?" he asked his daughter, trying his best to sound upbeat about it. In reality, he was dreading the event with a passion. All of LA was going to be there... all the people he hated, especially his own family. Nothing was more unappealing to him than knowing that he was going to be spending Friday night at a boring Hollywood event socializing with his ex-wife that he was still in love with, her punk of a new boyfriend, and his pregnant new wife that he wished he had never married. How fun could it possibly be?

"Be at Mom's house by four-thirty," she said, pleased that he was coming. "I want everyone to get there early so that we can take family pictures."

"I'll see you then," Peter said in disbelief as he pulled into his driveway. With that, they both clicked off. *Family pictures?* Surely Allison was joking. Somehow he knew she wasn't though.

"Seriously," he said in frustration as he parked his Porsche. Sometimes he didn't know what kept him off drugs.

Chapter 10

Elizabeth and Cameron decided to go to Vinny's Steak House for a late lunch. It was one of their favorite restaurants.

"Do you need a table for two?" the slender, attractive-looking hostess asked them, her soft voice enough to drive any man wild. For a second, Cameron couldn't help but be a little jealous. She didn't know why, though. She looked just as good as the hostess did, probably better.

"Yes, please," Elizabeth said.

"Follow me," the hostess said with a smile, showing off her perfect teeth. She led them to a small table in the back corner of the restaurant. There was no one else around.

"Will this do?" she asked.

"This is perfect," Elizabeth said enthusiastically, taking her seat. Cameron sat across from her.

"It better be perfect," they heard a friendly male voice say to the hostess. It was Antonio, their favorite waiter. "Elizabeth Herrington is one of our best customers," he continued. "She comes in here at least three times a week."

The hostess smiled and hurried off.

"Her name is Amanda," Antonio informed Elizabeth and Cameron, a wistful look in his eye. "I've been trying to get a date with her for over a month now. She's the only girl who's ever turned me down."

Somehow Elizabeth found this hard to believe. Antonio was charming, but not *that* charming.

"You'll probably get her eventually," Cameron said with a smile, secretly wishing he'd make a move on her.

"Maybe," Antonio sighed. "You never know. Women are just so unpredictable these days."

Elizabeth hid a smile. Everything about Antonio was hilarious to her.

"Are you two ready to order?"

"I'm not sure what I want yet," Cameron said, scanning the menu. "It's all always so good, it's hard for me to decide."

"I'll check back in a few minutes then, my friends," Antonio said, quickly walking over to an elderly couple who had just been seated across the room.

"He's so funny," Cameron whispered to her mother.

"That he is," Elizabeth said, eyeing herself in her compact mirror. She was reapplying her makeup. She looked great as she was, but she wanted to make sure of it.

Cameron's cell phone rang.

"Hello," she answered cheerfully, recognizing the number as being Allison's.

"Cameron, where are you?" Allison asked, her voice panicky. "I need to talk to you right away. It's really important."

Elizabeth could tell by the expression on her daughter's face that something was terribly wrong.

"What's wrong?" Elizabeth whispered. "What's going on?" Cameron held up a hand for her to be quiet.

"I'm at Vinny's. What's wrong?" she asked Allison, who was now sobbing into the phone.

"I need to tell you in person," her friend struggled to say. "It's too horrible to say over the phone. You're not going to believe this."

"Did you and Carter break up?" Cameron asked, praying that Carter hadn't dumped her the day of the premiere.

Elizabeth was listening intently. She hoped nothing was wrong with Peter.

"No, we didn't break up," Allison said, finally gaining control of her sobs.

"Then what?" Cameron demanded, completely bewildered and beginning to panic. What in the world could have happened in the last few hours? Allison had been in a great mood when she talked to her earlier."

"I need to tell you in person," her stepsister said again. "It's just too terrible to say over the phone."

"Where are you?" Cameron asked. "Is someone with you? Is Carter there?"

"No, I'm by myself. I'm at the house. Please hurry! I'm supposed to be meeting my mom and John for a late lunch at Villa Blanca in an hour."

"I can't come right now," Cameron said. "I'm with my mom here at Vinny's."

"Your mom is with you," Allison exclaimed, her voice becoming even more panicky. "Don't tell her how upset I am. Whatever you do, don't tell her."

Cameron was beginning to feel very nervous. Something was really, really wrong. Allison never acted like this.

"What's wrong?" Elizabeth whispered again.

Cameron didn't respond to her mother.

"Please tell me what's wrong, Allison?" she pleaded, beginning to cry herself. "Just tell me what's wrong."

Elizabeth had a worried look on her face.

"I didn't want to tell you this soon," Allison said, sobbing uncontrollably again. "I didn't want to ruin my movie coming out. I didn't want this to happen. This wasn't supposed to happen..." Her voice trailed off.

"Tell me, Allison," Cameron yelled into her cell phone. "Tell me what's going on!" The elderly couple who was sitting at the table across the room was now staring in her direction."

"I'm pregnant, Cameron!" Allison screamed, choking on the words. "I'm fucking pregnant." She was wailing now.

Feeling dizzy, Cameron grabbed the edge of the table to prevent herself from falling over.

"Pregnant," she said in disbelief, her voice barely above a whisper. "You're pregnant?"

Elizabeth gasped, her hands flying to her mouth. She was shaking her head disapprovingly. She wasn't surprised. Allison had always been a wild child and it looked like it had finally caught up with her.

"I'll be home in a few minutes," Cameron said, quickly clicking off. Elizabeth clasped her daughter's hands from across the table.

"Oh, Cameron," she moaned. "I can't believe this. I just can't believe it."

Cameron grabbed her purse and stood up to leave.

"Don't tell anyone about this, Mom," she said. "Not even Peter. It's not your responsibility to tell him. He and everyone else will find out soon enough." She paused. "Can I trust you to keep this quiet?"

Elizabeth nodded, seemingly in a daze. She was still digesting the news.

"I guess we better hurry and get home right now," she said.

"Yeah, if that's okay with you," Cameron said. "She really needs me. I've never seen her so upset." She looked at Elizabeth.

"Of course it's okay with me," Elizabeth said, grabbing her purse off the back of her chair. "Let's go."

"Is Carter the father?" she asked.

"I'm sure he is," Cameron said. "He's the only guy I know of who Allison's been dating lately."

Antonio walked up at the exact moment they were about to leave. He was grinning from ear to ear.

"Are my favorite two women ready for me to take their order yet?" he asked, giving Elizabeth a not so discreet wink.

"Something's come up and we're going to have to run," Elizabeth said to Antonio. He could tell that both Elizabeth and Cameron appeared to be frantic.

"Okay," he said, not feeling that it was his place to ask them what was wrong. "I hate you didn't get to stay and eat. I hope you come back soon."

"Oh, we will, Antonio," Elizabeth said, tossing a twenty down on the table. She was leaving a tip because she felt bad that she and Cameron were just running out like this after they had already been seated.

As Antonio made his way back to the kitchen, he wondered where they were rushing off to. He hoped something wasn't wrong with Cameron. She was one of the hottest girls he had ever seen. Not as hot as her stepsister Allison Herrington was, though. Allison was a total babe. *She* was the one he had his eyes on.

Antonio decided not to worry about the Herrington's anymore today. It wasn't going to do him any good to worry. He wasn't going to be able to figure out what was going on anyway. It could be anything. There was always something going on around here.

"This is one crazy town," he muttered to himself. "One crazy town."

Chapter 11

John Parker was waiting impatiently outside Villa Blanca. He was definitely not in a good mood. The last thing he felt like doing right now was having lunch with Harmon and Allison. Attending the get-together and premiere tonight was going to be bad enough. Wasn't that enough for one day? Was it really necessary that they all spend this much time together?

Of course, he could never tell Harmon how he felt about this. She would be furious about his unwillingness to spend time with them and would never let him hear the end of it. With all of the pressure he was under to finish writing his script, a war at home was the last thing he needed. Therefore, he was going to keep his mouth shut and pretend like everything was great. Hopefully it wouldn't be too bad anyway. Maybe if he just ignored Harmon and only talked to Allison, the meal would be halfway pleasant.

John's cell phone rang. He saw it was Harmon calling.

"Hello," he answered, thankful it wasn't the mysterious caller calling to ruin his day. On second thought, though, anybody would have probably been better than Harmon.

"Hey John," she said, sounding depressed, which he found to be very odd considering that she had been on a high about Allison's premiere only a few minutes earlier. "We're going to have to take a rain check on lunch. Allison just called me and said she's sick. She's throwing up over at her dad's house. Cameron's with her."

John raised his eyebrows. Allison had seemed fine when he talked to her earlier in the day. He wondered if something was up.

"That's okay," he said into his phone. "I hope she gets to feeling better before tonight."

"I'm sure she will," Harmon said, not sounding confident about it at all.

"Where are you right now?" John asked her, hoping she wasn't at home. He wanted to go back there and put in a few solid hours working on his screenplay.

"I'm in bed at home," she said.

Damn, he thought to himself. It was almost impossible for him to get away from her for long.

"I'll see you in a few minutes then," he said, walking back to his BMW. With that, he clicked off. Just as John got into his car, his cell phone rang again.

"Shit," he said aloud when the words 'private call' flashed across his phone. It was his tormenter. This was the first time he had heard from him in several days.

"What do you want?" John answered irritably, not trying at all to hide his anger.

"To congratulate you, of course," the voice said. "To congratulate you and your girlfriend, Ms. Herrington."

John began to back his BMW out of its parking place. He was tired of this guy playing mind games with him.

"Watch out!" the voice on the phone yelled. John slammed on his breaks. He had almost backed into a Jaguar. The woman driving the vehicle blew her horn at him.

"That was close," the caller said. "You need to be more careful with your driving."

John jumped out of his car. The caller was somewhere right around here! Whoever he was, he was watching John right now, right at this very moment.

"Where are you?" John raged into his phone. "Where the hell are you?" The caller didn't say anything. He just sat there, breathing into the phone. It was very, very eerie.

"Show yourself to me!" John yelled. "Be a man." He was spinning around, his eyes darting in every direction, but there didn't seem to be anyone in sight besides a few golfers here and there. The parking lot was virtually empty.

"I have to go," the caller suddenly said. "I'm late for an appointment. Congratulations again, though."

"Congratulations for what?" John asked, completely bewildered and frustrated by this entire situation. Why was he being congratulated?

"For Allison's victory, of course," the caller said. "She deserves to be a movie star. She's such a beautiful young woman." He paused. "Almost as beautiful as your Kelly was."

John's throat went dry. He had hoped the caller wouldn't ever bring up his late wife, Kelly, or the girls again.

"Do you want to know how I know about Kelly?" the caller laughed, sounding more evil than ever. "Do you?" He was laughing hysterically now. "The answer to that question is simple, John," he said, bringing his cold voice down almost to a whisper. "I'm the one who killed her," he bragged. "I killed your wife and your daughters, and got away with murder."

Chapter 12

The two men burst through the front door of the Herrington mansion. They were carrying machine guns and had wild, frantic looks in their eyes. Both men were unshaven and completely disheveled-looking.

"Allison, where are you?" one of them yelled out as he made his way up the grand staircase to the upper level. The second guy stayed on the main level to make sure Allison didn't try to escape.

The man who went upstairs was running from room to room looking for her. He found her in the bathroom, where she was curled up in a corner scared and crying. She had crawled there to hide when she heard the men burst through the front door. She didn't have a clue who these men were or what their motive was.

"Who are you?" she shrieked, completely panicked and terrified. "What do you want with me?"

"You don't know me, bitch," the guy sneered. "But I bet if you think hard enough, you can figure out who I work for."

Allison's face went white as she thought about it. Once it all came together in her mind, she knew she wasn't going to live. These men were here to kill her. The second guy was in the bathroom now as well. He'd heard the yelling and ran upstairs to help his associate.

"Please don't kill me," Allison pleaded. Her desperation was evident in her eyes. "I'm pregnant. You'll be killing the baby too, and the baby is innocent."

"Shut the fuck up," the guy yelled, shattering the bathroom mirror with his fist. "I could care less about the baby inside of you. You shouldn't have gone and got yourself knocked up."

Allison had never been this terrified before. She knew she was about to meet her fate, and there wasn't anything she could do to change the situation. Instinctively, she started crying hysterically. She couldn't believe things were going down like this.

"I don't want to die," she stammered. "I'm only nineteen-years-old. I've got my whole life ahead of me. I have so much to live for."

The two men just sneered at her.

"If you wanted to live, then you shouldn't have pissed off the wrong people. You knew that wasn't going to lead to anywhere good."

With that, he aimed the machine gun at Allison's head and started firing, spraying her with bullets. She was dead instantly. Allison Herrington, aspiring actress and one of the most popular girls in Beverly Hills, had been murdered and was now lying lifeless on the floor in a pool of her own blood.

Chapter 13

It was approaching one in the morning, but things at Joey's Bar were in full swing. Friday nights at the hot spot were always the best and tonight seemed even wilder than usual. The music was blaring, everyone was dancing, and the alcohol was flowing.

Carter Greenfield, the roommate of Steven Herrington and boyfriend of Allison Herrington, was sitting at the bar, where he was chugging his ninth beer of the evening. Carter, a mischievous twenty-year-old with dark brown skin and hazel eyes, was putting his fake ID to good use. A regular on the club scene, he lived for exciting nights like this one. Joey, the overweight owner of the bar, was busy mixing drinks behind the counter.

"Where's Steven tonight?" Joey asked Carter, trying to make conversation. Carter and Steven hardly ever came to the bar without each other. They were both roommates and drinking buddies.

"He said he didn't feel like partying," Carter responded, shrugging his shoulders. He had to speak loudly so that he could be heard above all the noise. "The premiere for *Deceptive Intentions* was tonight," he said. "I think he was going to that. His sister is starring in it."

Joey raised his eyebrows.

"Oh really," he said. "She must be a real looker."

Carter shook his head in disgust.

"She's a real bitch is what she is," he said, cracking open another beer. Feeling dizzy, he paused for a few seconds. The alcohol was definitely taking its effect on him. "If anyone should know about her, I should," he added. "She's my girlfriend."

Joey laughed. He could tell by the way Carter was slurring his speech that he had had *way* too much to drink.

"How come you've never told me you dated Herrington's sister?" he asked, fixing his eyes on a cheap-looking blonde who was dancing nearby.

Carter shrugged his shoulders again.

"Dunno," he said, looking down at the floor. "I don't like to talk about Allison very much. There's nothing good to say about her. She's the stuck-up Beverly Hills type. High maintenance, I guess you could say. I'm going to break up with her soon."

"So her name's Allison?" Joey asked, not backing off. He was trying to find out more about this girl. Maybe if Steven would introduce her to him, he could offer her a job here. He was always on the lookout for new strippers, and an actress type would definitely make the guys come running.

Carter nodded. "Allison Herrington," he said, lighting up a cigarette.

"Excuse me," interrupted a cute brunette with a perfect figure. Her voice was a little raspy. "Did you just say something about Allison Herrington?"

"Yeah," Carter answered, giving her a big smile. This girl was stunning. She was even better looking than his favorite stripper, Amber, who at the moment was giving a drunk college guy a lap dance across the room.

"Do you know Allison?" he asked, blowing smoke in the air.

"No," the girl said. "I just recognized her name."

"Recognized her name?" Carter pressed wanting to know more. Allison *was* an actress, but she wasn't well known yet.

"Yeah," she said, looking slightly confused. "Isn't she that girl starring in *Deceptive Intentions*? You know…the one who was killed earlier tonight?"

Chapter 14

The entire Herrington family was gathered in the oversized living room at Peter and Elizabeth's house in Beverly Hills. The entire family, except for Steven that is. There was no telling where *he* was.

No one in the room was saying much of anything. At this point no one really knew what to say. The last day and a half had been hell for them. Police officers and detectives coming in and out of their house asking all kinds of questions. Family and friends arriving with food and to express their condolences. It was all a blur.

Several questions were on the forefront of everyone's mind. Who had murdered Allison? And what was the reason for it? Who could possibly be capable of committing such a horrible crime? John wondered if it was her boyfriend, Carter Greenfield. Cameron had said that Allison had told him of her pregnancy only an hour before the get-together at Harmon's was set to begin. She had said that he'd been absolutely furious about it and had told her she needed to get an abortion. Allison had been devastated. She didn't want an abortion and had planned on keeping the baby. She had expected to have Carter's total support, and had been greatly surprised by his negative reaction.

The more John thought about it, the more he was becoming suspicious of Carter. After all, the boy was the last known person to have seen her alive and he *was* mad at her. He'd told the police that he'd stayed at Peter and Elizabeth's house after the rest of the family had left for Harmon's. He said he'd been talking to Allison about her pregnancy. She had been getting dressed for the party. He said that after getting into a huge argument with her, he'd left and driven out to Joey's Bar in the Valley. He was so pissed off he'd decided to just skip both the get together and the premiere.

John watched from his chair as Elizabeth tried to comfort Harmon, who was both grieving for Allison and feeling guilty. They were sitting on the small sofa across the room. Harmon felt guilty for not having known that her daughter was pregnant.

"This doesn't mean that you're not a good mother," Elizabeth said softly. "There's no way that you could have known that Allison was pregnant. She wasn't showing at all and wasn't displaying any other signs. It's not your fault."

"Elizabeth's right," Peter chimed in. He was sitting on the couch by the fireplace. "We can't blame ourselves. Allison shouldn't have been keeping her pregnancy from us. She knew better than to do something like that."

"Yeah Harmon," John agreed. "You can't blame yourself."

"Shut up," Harmon snapped at everyone, anger flashing in her eyes. "None of you know what you're talking about. None of you! She knew how I would react if she told me she was pregnant, and that's my fault. I should have been more understanding all these years. I'm her mother. She should have been able to come to me." Harmon was sobbing again. She was completely beside herself trying to deal with this.

"Who would have killed her?" she wailed, throwing herself on the floor. "Who would have done this to her?" She was crying hysterically now and flinging her arms. Elizabeth began to cry herself. As much as she disliked Harmon, she genuinely couldn't help but feel sorry for her. No one deserved to lose their daughter in this horrible way. It was unthinkable, completely unimaginable.

Cameron suddenly entered the room.

"Can I get anyone anything?" she asked, eyeing Harmon who was still on the floor crying. "I just made some coffee, if you'd like me to bring it in."

"That would be nice," John said, giving her a smile. He greatly appreciated all of Cameron and Elizabeth's efforts to make things easier for Harmon and Peter.

"I'll bring it right in then," Cameron said, leaving the room to walk back to the kitchen.

"I'll go help her," Elizabeth said, following behind her daughter. When she reached the kitchen, she found Cameron sitting at the table in the bay window, tears streaming down her face.

"Oh Mom," she cried. "What am I going to do?"

Elizabeth wrapped her arms around her daughter.

"You need to be strong," she said. "Allison would want you to be strong."

"No, Mom," Cameron said, beginning to cry even harder. "It's not Allison I'm crying about."

"What then?" Elizabeth asked, concern evident on her face. "What's wrong? What's the matter?"

Cameron buried her face in her hands.

"Allison's not the only one who messed around and got herself pregnant," she whispered, choking on her sobs. "I'm pregnant too." Elizabeth felt like she had been kicked in the stomach. There was a long pause.

"And do you want to know the worst part," she continued, wiping her tears. "Carter Greenfield is the father."

Chapter 15

John was sitting by himself in Peter and Elizabeth's small library on the second floor of their house. Wanting to be alone, he had come up here for a little while. He needed time to think, and this was the perfect place to do it. He liked everything about this room. It was small and tidy, with plenty of books. Being a writer, he always enjoyed spending time in libraries, even though he chose to write screenplays, not books. Another reason he had come up here was because this room was a stark contrast to the rest of the house, in which an overwhelming sense of grief was permeating. It seemed to be a happier room than the rest of the house. Two oval-shaped windows allowed sunlight to illuminate the room.

Just as John closed his eyes and was beginning to relax, his cell phone rang. He knew who it was before he even looked. It was the caller. He didn't know how he knew. He just did.

"Hello," he answered, trying his best to be patient. After the events of the last day and a half, he really wasn't in the mood to argue, even if it was with the killer of his wife and daughters.

"Hello, John," the caller chirped, obviously in a good mood. "I was just calling to see how you're holding up. I've been worried sick about you and the Herrington's ever since premiere night. A tragedy such as this is never welcome. Allison was such an innocent young girl." The tone of his voice was conveying nothing but sarcasm.

John was mad now.

"Your calls to me are completely and totally pointless," he raged. "We never talk about anything productive. You just want to torture me. You want to constantly remind me that you killed my family, and I don't understand why. Haven't you already done enough damage and caused me enough pain? What do you have against me?"

The caller just sat there without saying a word. At least ten seconds ensued.

"Killing Allison was a pleasure," he finally said, his voice sounding more evil than ever before. "Watching her die was an extremely gratifying experience. I wish you had been there to watch. It was like a horror movie come to life. You would have been thoroughly entertained."

John's body had gone cold. The caller's words were chilling him to the bone. He felt completely helpless. The man who had taken away his first family was wreaking destruction on the people who were in his life now, and there wasn't anything he could do about it.

"Why did you kill Allison?" John asked, his voice remaining calm. He felt too defeated to fight back. "What purpose is her death serving? Can you at least tell me that?" He was almost in tears.

The caller laughed. "You're so gullible, John," he said, his voice conveying full confidence. The caller felt invincible, and the tingling sensation it gave him was indescribable. "I didn't kill Allison," he continued, still enjoying the moment. "Eliminating her was never a part of my plan. I had nothing to do with her death and I honestly don't know who did. I was just messing with your mind. I love to mess with your mind."

John was instantly relieved. He wouldn't have been able to live with himself if he had somehow indirectly been the cause of Allison's death.

The caller coughed. "I will become one with you, John," he continued. "You have everything in your life that I want in my own. That's the way it's always been. You've always had more than me. Kelly was a beautiful woman and I deserved her. You didn't. You didn't deserve Grace and Molly either. That's why I had to kill them. I had to make sure you didn't stay happy forever." There was another long pause. "And just like you didn't deserve Kelly, you don't deserve Harmon either," he continued. "Harmon's time is coming if you continue to pursue her, John," the caller said. "You mark my words. Her time is coming. That's one promise you can count on me keeping." With those horrifying words, the call ended.

Chapter 16

Steven was lying low at the house in Malibu, strung out on cocaine and popping all kinds of pills. He wasn't doing the drugs to numb any pain he felt over the loss of his sister. He didn't really even feel that much sorrow because of Allison's death. It wasn't like he didn't have a heart. He just hadn't ever really been that close to her. Despite Steven's lack of grief, he still felt sorry for the kid. Dying in such a brutal way must have been horrible, which is why he knew for sure that he was going to personally kill whoever was behind her murder if he ever found out.

The reason Steven was this doped up was because the overwhelming sense of sadness he had felt in his father's house had finally sent him over the edge. He had spent the past couple of days at the Beverly Hills house to show support for his family, but now he was sick and tired of the whole thing. He was tired of everyone sitting around feeling sorry for each other. Inactivity and a never ending pity party weren't going to bring Allison back. It was high time his family realized that. The funeral was tomorrow, and he wasn't even going to attend. He hated funerals and always avoided them at all costs. This one was going to be no exception.

As he paced around the spacious living room which overlooked the ocean, Steven suddenly realized that he needed to get the house cleaned up. The place hadn't been cleaned in weeks and was absolutely filthy. He planned on going out to the bars tonight to try to find a hot girl to bring home with him. Three floors of dirtiness would definitely be a turnoff, and turning a girl away from him was the last thing he needed right now. After two days of constantly being around his controlling father and nutcase of a mother, he needed sex more than he ever had before.

Steven's parents pissed him off more than any two people he knew. They were both so judgmental of him and his, what they considered to be, unconventional lifestyle. So what if he did a little drugs and didn't go to college? Why should it bother them? Why were they dead set on wanting him to "clean up his life," get back in school, and "make something of himself"? What the hell did "make something of himself" mean anyway? Becoming a doctor or a lawyer was what they had in mind, but there was no way that was ever going to happen. He wasn't going to waste his life being boring like his parents. They were such losers, especially his father. Peter Herrington…plastic surgeon and father of three. Didn't the man want to be known for something a little more exciting. The only thing spontaneous his dad had ever done was get involved with Elizabeth, and just look how royally he had screwed that up now. The woman with killer looks was pregnant, and soon to be fat as a cow.

Steven had to give his mother a little more credit, however. As crazy as she was, she really did know how to spice things up in her life. He found that out two years ago when he had overheard a certain very interesting phone conversation his mother had had. He had never confronted her with what he knew about her, though. The way he looked at it, everyone was entitled to a little secret. Besides her one secret, though, she was just as boring as the rest of the Beverly Hills crowd. Life was an endless stream of overdone parties and awkward social gatherings with the rich and famous, all of whom were desperately trying to impress each other and be important. What a bunch of bumbling imbeciles. What all his parents' friends really needed was to get their noses out of the air and get over themselves. Steven was tired of all these jerks looking down on him when all he was doing was just being true to himself.

Suddenly feeling the need to be outdoors, Steven walked out on the deck to smoke a cigarette. The nicotine calmed him down after a few minutes, and he began thinking about later that night. He couldn't wait to find a girl to bring home with him. Every time he went out to the bars, the girls fell all over him, so he wouldn't have trouble finding one. Unlike his roommate, Carter, he could get any female he wanted. Steven didn't understand what his roommate's problem was.

Carter was always high and becoming more of a loser everyday. Now the poor guy was a total basket case because of Allison's death, and was talking about moving to Europe to get away from all the pain he had experienced in his life. He said that he needed to make a fresh start and forget his past. *Make a fresh start, Steven's ass.* What Carter needed was to get a new girl in his life and quit whining and complaining. It wasn't liked he and Allison would have worked out anyway. They weren't each other's type.

Finished smoking his cigarette, Steven lit another one and inhaled the smoke deep into his lungs. He gazed off the deck towards the ocean, trying to make sense of what had happened to Allison. For the life of him, he couldn't think of one single person who could have had such a huge grudge against her that they would go so far as to kill her. Allison was both very pretty and popular, and everyone liked her a lot. As far as he knew, she didn't have any enemies.

As he continued to think about the situation, his cell phone rang. It was his mother.

"Hello," he answered exasperatedly, annoyed that she was calling him.

"Cameron did it," Harmon shrieked into the phone, her wails ringing in his ears. "Cameron killed your sister!"

Chapter 17

Sitting across the kitchen table from Detective Walter Mason, who was asking her all kinds of questions, Elizabeth was absolutely terrified for her daughter. Cameron was in major trouble, and there wasn't a thing anyone could do to get her out of this situation. As her mother, Elizabeth desperately wished that there was something she could do, but there just wasn't. At this point, all she could do was try to help Cameron not get into any further trouble. She knew her daughter was innocent, but trying to convince the detectives of that wasn't going to be easy. Because Cameron had concealed the fact that she was pregnant, and that the father of the baby was her murdered stepsister's boyfriend, she didn't exactly look like the most trustworthy individual.

According to Cameron, who was being questioned by detectives in another part of the house, she had had a one night stand with Carter Greenfield five months ago. She had gone home with him one night after a party at one of their mutual friend's house in Pacific Palisades. Once they were back at Carter's place, one thing had led to another and she slept with him. About a month later she had discovered that she was pregnant. By that time, Carter and Allison were dating and Cameron hadn't wanted to spoil things for Allison by announcing that she was pregnant.

"I didn't know what to do, Mom," Cameron had sobbed to Elizabeth just a few hours ago. "So I just never told anyone. I wasn't showing any and even now no one can tell that I'm pregnant. You have no idea how hard this has been for me to keep this to myself. I've been so scared."

The harsh tone of Detective Mason's voice made Elizabeth jump. She could tell that he didn't like her.

"How close of a relationship do you have with your daughter?" he asked, his dark brown eyes studying her intently. A slightly overweight man with gray hair and a rapidly receding hairline, Mason had to be in his mid-sixties.

"Very close," Elizabeth answered. Her voice was shaky and her body was trembling with anxiety. "That's why I'm so shocked that Cameron hadn't already told me what was going on with her. We've always been so close and had such a good relationship. I just can't get over this." She paused. "Cameron's a good kid and always has been, Detective," she continued, trying her best to make him believe her. "Just because she made a mistake and kept her pregnancy a secret doesn't mean that she's a killer. Allison has been her best friend for years. They've always been like sisters and then they became stepsisters. There's no way that Cameron would ever have done anything like this. I'm positive of that."

"I don't know how you could be positive about anything concerning your daughter right now," Mason said coldly. "Considering what she admitted to us earlier, I, for one, have trouble believing *anything* she says. The girl is five months pregnant and hadn't yet told anyone about it until today."

Elizabeth was downright mad now. This man had been rude to her ever since she and Cameron had admitted Cameron's pregnancy to him a few hours ago and she was tired of it.

"How many times do I have to tell you?" she cried out. "She was scared! Surely you can understand that. It's scary enough to be nineteen and pregnant, but to be nineteen and pregnant under these circumstances is so much worse. If Cameron had admitted who the father of the baby was, she could have lost her lifelong best friend over it."

"I don't understand why you're getting so defensive Mrs. Herrington," Mason said, looking at her scornfully.

"Because you're trying to make Cameron out to be some cheap little whore, and I'm not going to stand for it. She made a mistake, but let me say again, in no way does that make her a murderer. You think that she killed Allison so that she could get Carter to herself since she was pregnant, and that's just not the case. Cameron has no long-term romantic interest in Carter and would never pursue a relationship with a boy she wasn't in love with. She's not that desperate."

"Well, excuse me," Mason piped up, his voice full of sarcasm. "What am I *supposed* to think. She *is* pregnant and the father of the baby *is* the boyfriend of her murdered stepsister."

Elizabeth was shaking with fury at this point.

"How dare you say it that way," she yelled, her face fiery red. "You make it sound like she slept with Carter while Allison was dating him and that's not what happened. She slept with him before he started dating Allison. Like I said before, you're trying to make her out to be a whore, and you're not going to get away with it. Eventually the real truth is going to come out and then you'll be sorry for treating me this way."

"I'm fully aware that Cameron slept with Carter before he began dating Allison," Mason said. "I didn't intentionally mean to make it sound any other way." He was still looking at her scornfully. "And for Cameron's sake, I hope that you're right and that there is another explanation for what happened to Allison. I have a feeling, however, that the real truth is already right here in front of us and that you just can't see it."

Realizing that she wasn't going to convince Mason that he was wrong, Elizabeth got her cell phone out of her purse.

"I'm going to call my lawyer," she said. "I think this is all getting a little out of control."

Chapter 18

Sitting in a chair all by himself in the lavish master bedroom of his mansion, Peter Herrington was feeling miserable and wished that he could escape his problems. He was tired of having so many people in the house all at once. What he wanted more than anything was to be alone, and to get some rest. He hadn't slept more than a few hours since the night before Allison's murder, so his body was fatigued and desperately craving sleep. Didn't all of his family's friends who either kept coming over or calling to check on them understand that they needed a break from this?

Not only was Peter tired of visiting with friends, he was also tired of answering questions from the detectives. They were getting on his nerves and seemed to be asking him the same questions over and over again. In addition to this, Peter also felt like the media was treating his family as prey. Because of Allison's newfound fame with *Deceptive Intentions*, which was now in theaters, the story of her death was the subject of every news program and national talk show. Reporters were calling the house repeatedly, pestering someone in the family to give an interview. Peter didn't understand why the media didn't accept that they were in the grieving process and didn't have the desire to talk to the public about the extreme sorrow they were feeling. He was sure that after Allison's funeral, someone in the family, most likely Harmon, would give an interview, but Peter knew that right now an interview was out of the question.

The funeral was planned for tomorrow morning at eleven o'clock at Forest Lawn. Peter expected the ceremony to be crowded because Allison had so many friends. Even though he and the rest of his family had a tremendous amount of support from the community, the thought that tomorrow he would be attending his own daughter's funeral made him almost physically ill. Parents weren't supposed to live to bury their children. This wasn't how it was supposed to be.

In addition to feeling grief, Peter also felt a little guilty. He wasn't quite sure why. For some reason, he felt like he had failed Allison as a father and that maybe he could have prevented this from happening if he had been more protective of her all these years. If Cameron *was* responsible for Allison's death, maybe he should have been more aware of what was going on within his own household. He knew that parental involvement was one of the main keys to keep teenagers out of trouble, so he knew that in a way this was his fault. Over the years, both he and Harmon had always been too focused on themselves to spend real quality time with Steven and Allison. In his heart, Peter knew that was why Steven had turned out the way he had. Even though he had spent some time with Steven as a child, they had never really experienced a close father-son bond. As far as Harmon went, however, she had never really paid any attention whatsoever to Steven, and the only time she had spent with Allison had been when she was grooming her to become the next big Hollywood actress. Maintaining high social status and achieving more and more fame were the only things that Harmon spent any amount of time on.

Peter had a feeling that even though Harmon seemed to be grief-stricken by Allison's death, she would eventually think of a way to make the media attention surrounding the murder work to her advantage. After the funeral, she would probably appear on all the popular talk shows, talking about the case in an effort to acquire more fame for herself. Knowing her, she would probably even try to get a book or movie deal out of it.

Peter had already contacted the hit man he had hired to kill Harmon and told him to postpone committing the deed. With all the police detectives milling around him and his family, Peter was certain he would get caught if he followed through with the plan. Spending the rest of his life in federal prison wasn't exactly what he envisioned for his future. Besides, he really wasn't sure that he wanted Harmon dead anyway, so this postponement would give him time to think more about it. The only reason Peter had hired the hit man to begin with was because he had been trying to have Harmon killed before she had him killed. Surely she had postponed her plans also, though. Surely she wasn't actually stupid enough to go through with having him killed any time soon with all of these detectives around.

Ever since the private detective he had hired to trail her had told him that Harmon appeared to be planning on utilizing the services of renowned hit man, Leonard Holt, Peter had been convinced that she was in the process of plotting his demise. Before learning of Elizabeth's pregnancy, he could have cared less if he died so he really hadn't been that nervous about her plans. Now things were different, though. He had something to live for. He was going to be a father again and he had already vowed to himself that this time he was going to do everything different. He was going to be a good father and take an active role in raising the child. By doing things right this time, he could make up for all the ways he failed his other two kids. Because this was his second chance, he was going to have to be careful and make sure he would still be around to take advantage of the chance.

Since he still had the private detective following Harmon everywhere she went, Peter had full confidence that he would find out from him if she had anymore contact with Holt. If Peter was given any reason to believe that Harmon hadn't postponed her plans, he would go ahead and go through with having her eliminated. If he didn't ever get the idea that she was still planning on having him killed, he might even decide to never go through with his own plans.

Thinking about this, Peter suddenly felt slightly optimistic for the first time since Allison's death. Even though he knew he had failed both of his kids, especially his daughter, he had a feeling that everything was going to turn out completely different with his new child. It was a really good feeling that made him feel more at peace than he ever had before.

"This time I'm going to give fatherhood my all," he said aloud. "I'm going to give it everything I have."

"Well good for you," someone said coldly from behind him, just as Peter felt a gun being shoved up against the back of his head. The words were spoken by a voice filled with sarcasm, resentment, and malice. He recognized it as being the voice of Harmon. Too shocked to even yell for help, Peter just sat there, not saying a word, completely terrified for his life.

"I'm glad to see you've become such a big family man," she continued, pressing the gun even harder against the back of his head. "But before you make anymore plans for the future, the two of us need to have a little chat."

Chapter 19

With Harmon still holding him at gunpoint, Peter finally worked up the courage to say something. He chose his words carefully, however.

"What is this about, Harmon?" he asked her, trying not to allow the complete and utter terror he felt to be evident in his voice. She was still standing behind him, so he couldn't see her, which made his situation all the more terrifying.

"Oh, I just think that we're long overdue for a good chat," she answered him. "It's been a long time since we've sat down together and had a good heart to heart." She sounded deranged and completely unhinged. Peter knew she wasn't, though. She wasn't mentally unstable at all. She knew exactly what she was doing. She was a very calculating and manipulative woman who would go to any length to get what she wanted. This was her way of doing just that. The only thing that surprised Peter about this was that she was doing it with so many detectives present downstairs.

Peter could still feel the gun pushed to his head.

"What exactly is it that you want to talk about?" he asked, choosing his words carefully. He knew he better not misspeak because he was beginning to think that Harmon was crazy enough to shoot him right here and now if she felt inclined to do so.

"I want to talk about what happened to Allison," she said. "And I want to talk about what we're going to do about Cameron."

"Well, why don't you put the gun down first," Peter suggested. "I don't feel comfortable talking to you with you holding a gun to my head."

"I'll put it down, Peter, but if you yell out or try to run for help, I *will* kill you. You mark my words. I will kill you right here, right now. I'm not afraid of going to prison."

"Don't worry, I'm not going to try anything," Peter said truthfully. He was too curious to hear what she had to say to try to get help. "Why don't you take a seat," he said, motioning to the chair next to him.

Harmon kept the gun in her hands, however she took a seat like Peter had suggested. He was instantly relieved that she was no longer pointing the weapon at him. Now that she was sitting in the chair next to him, he was amazed at how stunningly attractive she looked even under these circumstances. Even though she wasn't wearing any makeup and looked like she hadn't slept in three days, she still had the ability to drive him wild. There had always been something that lured him to her and made him want her more than he had ever wanted any-one else. Divorcing her was his biggest regret even though they were toxic to each other, and their entire marriage had been a rollercoaster ride from hell.

"What do you *want* us to do about Cameron?" Peter finally asked her after they had both stared at each other for about a minute without saying a word. "What can we do? Shouldn't we just sit back and let the authorities do their work?"

"I guess that depends on how far you're willing to go," Harmon responded, her sharp black eyes piercing his. "And how dedicated you are to making sure the little murderer winds up either behind bars or dead."

Peter wasn't surprised by what he heard. He should have known that Harmon would want to take the law into her own hands.

"I don't want to kill her," he said definitively. "She's my stepdaughter. I want to do what I can to make sure that she goes to prison, but as far as I can see, my role in that capacity is going to be very limited."

"Oh, that's where you're wrong," Harmon lashed out, glaring viciously at him, her body trembling with rage. "You're going to stand up for your daughter and family and do the right thing for once in your miserable life whether you like it or not. You're going to help me in doing everything you possibly can to put Cameron behind bars—legal or not."

"What do you mean, legal or not?" Peter asked, secretly impressed with Harmon's determination but wishing that she wasn't so headstrong and willing to take such drastic measures. He really didn't think it was a wise idea for them to take matters into their own hands.

"I mean exactly what I said," she answered him, still in a rage. "We're going to do our very best to make sure the crazy girl goes to jail, and if that doesn't work, then we're going to kill her. And when I say everything, believe me, I *do* mean everything. If the police don't get enough evidence against her to convict her, then we're going to do everything we can to, in essence, *create* evidence against her. We're not going to play fair. We will lie like hell to the police about Cameron until they finally feel confident enough to arrest her."

Peter sighed and shook his head. Even though he admired Harmon's willpower, he didn't agree with what she was saying.

"Harmon, I wish you would take a moment to really think about what you're proposing," he said slowly, trying to put it delicately. "If we lie to the police, then we're going to wind up in prison along with Cameron."

Harmon had calmed down by this point and was doing everything she desperately could to keep her cool.

"Like I said just a few minutes ago, I'm not afraid in the least of going to prison," she said. "Cameron needs to pay for what she did to Allison and if I have to sacrifice my freedom to bring about justice, then so be it."

"What if you're wrong?" Peter asked her, trying to rationalize with his ex-wife. "What if Cameron isn't the person who killed Allison?

Wouldn't you feel guilty if because of your lies and manipulations, an innocent girl winds up spending the rest of her life in prison?"

"Cameron Simms is *not* an innocent girl," Harmon snapped at him, losing her temper once again. "She's a very, very evil girl and is definitely the person who did this." She was waving her hands, along with the gun, in the air in exasperation. "Everyone knows she did it," Harmon continued, the tone of her voice conveying contempt. "You really need to jump on board here and help me out. I need all the help I can get making sure she goes down for this."

Peter still wasn't so sure about it. He had a nagging feeling that Cameron might not be the one who did this, and that someone else was responsible. He would really feel better leaving the law in the hands of the police, especially since he was married to Elizabeth and didn't want to make things any harder for her than they already were.

"Let me ask you this," he said calmly, again choosing his words carefully since Harmon still had the gun in her hands. "What are you going to do if I don't agree to help you out? What are you going to do then?"

Harmon gave him a sly smile but it was a smile that made him shiver. "I'll kill you," she said icily, her words chilling him to the bone. "It's as simple as that."

Chapter 20

Wearing a black Armani suit, John Parker walked out of the church in Beverly Hills hand in hand with Harmon, who was smiling and doing remarkably well, considering she had just attended her own daughter's funeral. Even though she was grieving for Allison, right now she was focused more on all of the reporters surrounding the church than she was on her loss. She loved attention more than anything else in the world.

The couple was instantly blinded by what seemed like hundreds of flashing camera lights from the many photographers frantically snapping their picture. John felt overwhelmed as he led Harmon through the crowd of media to his BMW, which was parked at the curb directly in front of the church. He knew she must be feeling the same way with all the reporters yelling questions at them.

"When are the police going to arrest Cameron Simms?" he heard one yell out.

"Ms. Herrington, how did you and your ex-husband not know that Allison was pregnant?" another one had the guts to ask, just as John was helping Harmon into the vehicle. Neither one of them responded to any of the questions.

"Are you ready?" John asked her once he too was inside the car. He shot a glance in her direction.

"Yes, I'm ready, you moron," she snapped as the funeral procession began moving in the direction of Forest Lawn Memorial Park, the cemetery where Allison was going to be buried. A graveside service was set to begin in half an hour.

For the next few minutes, the couple drove in silence. Harmon's behavior toward John had rapidly deteriorated the past few days, and he greatly resented it. She had been treating him badly for several months now, making fun of his screenplay and lack of a source of income, but the berating was at an all time high now. The only reason he didn't go ahead and end their relationship was because he felt too sorry for her to leave her alone right now. As hateful and spiteful as she was, he knew he didn't have the heart to go so far as to do that to her, even though that was exactly what she deserved.

Just because she was upset and grieving for Allison didn't give her the right to mistreat him. He was a person too and had been good to her this past year. Sure, he wasn't a millionaire like she was used to, but he had tried to provide her with love and support, which is something she had never really had before. Her relationship with Peter had been more like an obsession than true love. There had been nothing normal about their marriage at all. It had been nothing but a twenty- year-long rocky road of highs and lows that would have driven any normal person insane.

What John didn't understand was why Harmon didn't want to experience true love. Why didn't she want a relationship with a man who truly cared about her? Why did she constantly berate him when he was the only person in the entire world who seemed to care anything about her? Before he had finally wised up and seen how completely evil she actually was, John had really loved her. When he had first met her last year, her divorce from Peter had just been finalized. He had seen in her a deeply hurt woman desperately yearning for something more in her life. He thought he could replace the void in her life with love, but he was wrong. No matter how much affection he had shown her, it had never been enough. All she cared about was fame and money, both of which he didn't have. As far as Harmon was concerned, all the love in the world wasn't enough to replace fame and money.

Her voice interrupted John's thoughts.

"Elizabeth looked horrible at the church," she said aloud, more to herself than to him. "Her dress was hideous."

John disagreed. He thought Elizabeth looked very nice, and was really impressed with how much she had been reaching out to Harmon these past few days in an attempt to provide comfort. He didn't say anything, however, because he didn't want to argue with Harmon. It wasn't like it would do any good for him to say anything. It didn't matter what Elizabeth did, Harmon was never going to like her because she was Peter's trophy wife and had taken over her role as Mrs. Herrington…not to mention the fact that she was Cameron's mother.

"What the hell is wrong with you?" she snapped at John, turning in her seat to face him. His silence had led her to believe that he didn't agree with her. "Do you not think I'm right? I mean, surely you don't have such bad taste that you think she actually looked good?" She paused. "Well, I take that back. I guess you do have bad taste. I forgot about all the bimbos you dated before you met me."

John didn't have any idea what she was talking about. He had dated several different women since he'd arrived in LA, but none of them were bimbos.

"I never dated any bimbos, Harmon," he said, trying to keep his cool, even though he could feel anger welling up inside him. "And I don't really think it matters how anyone is dressed today. This is a funeral, not a fashion show."

She would have argued with him more if they weren't already getting close to the cemetery. John could tell that she was too nervous about what was going to happen when they got there to argue anymore. He could feel himself getting a little jittery too. There was probably going to be a lot of media present. John understandably didn't like the media after everything that happened to him back in Atlanta. His biggest fear was that with all of these reporters around, someone was going to somehow recognize him as being Neil Hudson, and then he would be exposed as a liar to everyone in his new life. As the procession approached the cemetery, John was completely shocked by what he saw. The scene awaiting them was a total circus. It made the reporters who had swarmed them outside the church look tame. A dozen or more news vans lined both sides of the road, and reporters and photographers were everywhere, literally surrounding the vehicles as they got closer to the entrance of the cemetery. There were even three helicopters churning overhead, all three of which were filled with media.

"Well, I'll be damned," Harmon said. "This just might be my big career break."

Chapter 21

Steven was sitting at the crowded bar at Joey's Bar. It seemed like Joey's was the only club he went out to these days, or at least enjoyed going out to. He and some of his Beverly Hills buddies had been out the past couple of weeks to some of the nicer clubs, but he hadn't really enjoyed himself. Those places just weren't his thing anymore…neither were those buddies. They were a little too Hollywood for his tastes.

As he took a sip of his Jack and Coke and scanned the noisy, packed-out club for hot girls, Steven came to the realization that his wild nights of partying at the celebrity-filled hotspots along Sunset Strip and Hollywood Boulevard were over. He didn't have a desire for it anymore. Come to think of it, he had never had a desire for it. He had just hung out in those places because that's where all his friends hung out. He preferred the laid-back atmosphere at Joey's, and he especially preferred the girls. They were more down to earth, or at least that's how he liked to think of them. In reality, he knew that most of them were trashy and cheap-looking, but hell, that's how he liked them anyway.

Steven was half-turned around on the barstool eyeing the strippers, who were dancing provocatively across the room. He was especially checking out Amber, his favorite one. Everything about her turned him on.

"Hey Stevo," he suddenly heard someone yell at him over the deafeningly loud music. He turned around to see Joey leaning across the bar at him. His face was red and perspiration was visible on his forehead. Joey and three other bartenders had been working hard making drinks all night. "That girl you were talking to in here a few weeks ago just walked in," he said.

"Which girl are you talking about?" Steven asked. He had talked to probably a hundred or more girls in here the past few weeks, even took a few of them home with him. How was he supposed to remember which one Joey was referring to?

"That Samantha chick," Joey said impatiently. "Samantha Taylor. You know, the one you blew it with." Steven's heart sped up. He knew who Joey was talking about now. This was the girl he wanted to get with really bad…the one Joey had given him hell about when she ditched him at the club a few weeks ago.

"Yeah, I remember her," he said to Joey, spotting her dancing across the room with the same group of hot blond girlfriends she was with the last time he had talked to her. Samantha and her friends were attracting a lot of attention and had basically every guy in the place drooling over them. Steven wondered who they were and why they were hanging out at a place like Joey's. These girls were more like girls he'd see partying at one of the trendy Hollywood clubs. He also wondered why he was attracted to Samantha. Sure she looked good, but he usually went for the cheap-looking girls, and Samantha definitely didn't fit that description.

"Get me another Jack and Coke," Steven said to Joey, lighting up a cigarette. Joey gave him a disgusted look.

"I can't believe you're still sitting here," he groaned. "You're not even gonna go talk to her."

"I'm going to," Steven said, making sure his voice sounded cocky. "I just want to have another drink first. And I'll tell you what else I'm gonna do," he bragged. "I'm gonna have her all over me by the end of the night."

"Now that's my man," Joey laughed. He hurried off to make the drink.

In reality, Steven wasn't sure if he was going to go over and try to talk to her or not. He wanted to think about it for a few minutes. She had blown him off last time, and girls who blew Steven Herrington off usually didn't get a second chance. He wasn't given anymore time to think, however. Samantha was at his side a second later, rubbing up against him. She had a big smile on her face.

"Well, look who it is," she cooed, batting her baby blue eyes at him. "If it isn't Mr. Herrington, the big player himself." As much as Steven wanted to, he didn't walk away. He knew that no matter how hard he tried, he wasn't going to be able to resist this girl. She was too hot. The sexiest thing about her was that she was so mysterious. It drove him fucking wild. Who was she? Where had she come from?

He flashed a big smile and gave her a little wink.

"What's up, Samantha?" he asked offhandedly, inhaling smoke from the cigarette down into his lungs. "How have you been?"

Joey returned with the Jack and Coke, but rushed off without saying anything. He had too many customers to deal with to keep standing around talking. Steven hadn't failed to notice the discreet thumbs up he had given him when he saw that he was talking to Samantha, however.

"I've been very good," she said, still standing up but leaning in close to him. There wasn't an available barstool for her to sit down, and Steven wasn't about to give up his seat to her. He didn't want to appear too accommodating. "How about yourself?" she asked. She talked softly to him to tease him.

"Not too bad," Steven said, shrugging his shoulders. "Not too bad." He put out his cigarette in the ashtray in front of him and lit up another one.

"I bet you'd be doing a lot better if you got what you wanted," Samantha said, still giving him a big smile.

"What are you talking about?" he asked, turning to face her. He was genuinely confused.

"You want me, Steven. I'm what you want, and I hope you don't think I don't know that." She was staring directly into his eyes, fully confident in herself. He could barely hear her because the music was still blasting. "And you want to know something?" she said, still leaning in close to him. "You just might get me one day if you wish hard enough." With that, she got up to leave. Steven was speechless. He couldn't believe this girl. Who did she think she was teasing him like this?

"Oh, and one last thing," she said, giving him a wink that made him wonder if she was mocking how he'd winked at her a few minutes before. "I won't be back in here for a few weeks, so ask Joey how to get in touch with me if you feel the need."

Steven gave her a blank look.

"Joey?" he asked, completely confused. "How the hell is Joey going to get me in touch with you? He says he hardly even knows you."

"That's just what he wants you to think, Steven," she said, still smiling at him. "And do you want to know why he wants you to think that? Because that's what we agreed we should make you think. It's all been a lie, though. Joey knows me quite well. He's my uncle."

Chapter 22

It was almost midnight, and Steven was sitting outside smoking a cigarette on his balcony at his condominium in West Hollywood. He had decided to spend the night here because he didn't feel like driving all way back to Malibu. The condo was on Doheny just off the Sunset Strip. Many celebrities lived in the high rise, which is why he preferred spending most of his time at the beach house. He was sick and tired of being around celebrities, and desperately craved a more normal life.

His parents had bought the condo for him for his birthday a few years ago. It was before they divorced. Steven was still living at the Beverly Hills house at the time, so they'd just been trying to get him out of the house. Back in those days, he had still very much been living the young Hollywood lifestyle, so he had loved the place. It was decorated in a very masculine way, and was the ultimate bachelor pad.

Steven especially loved the large balcony off of his living room, where he was sitting right now. He was trying to make sense of what he had learned earlier in the night at Joey's Bar. For once, he wasn't drinking. He wanted to be able to think clearly so that he could figure this out.

Why in the world had Joey pretended like he hadn't any idea who Samantha Taylor was when she was really his niece? Steven asked himself again, taking a drag on his cigarette. It didn't make any sense. He had known Joey for years now, and considered him a friend. Now he wasn't so sure. With all the out of control media publicity surrounding his sister's murder, he didn't know who he could trust. If the Samantha Taylor shenanigans hadn't begun before Allison was killed, Steven would have come to the conclusion that Joey was getting his niece to seduce him so that she could spend time with him and later sell information about him to the tabloids. Samantha had first spoken to him before Allison was killed, though. Steven kept thinking, trying to come up with another possibility, but nothing came to mind.

He had thought about confronting Joey about it as soon as Samantha told him, but he decided against it. He decided that it wouldn't do him any good to confront him. Since Joey went to all this trouble to conceal his relationship to Samantha, Steven knew that he wasn't going to admit what he and his niece were up to. Steven knew that the best way for him to get to the bottom of what was going on was to investigate this on his own. Maybe by playing detective, he would even get to know Samantha a little better. Kill two birds with one stone.

Steven took another drag on his cigarette. Even though he knew that Samantha was up to something, he still wanted to sleep with her. He wasn't going to quit pursuing her until he had done just that. He was used to getting what he wanted, and wasn't going to give up on her just because she was playing hard to get. Besides, he knew that she wanted him to pursue her. She was enjoying teasing him, and he had to admit to himself that he loved the chase. Most of the other girls he'd been with had been easy to get in bed, but Samantha wasn't like that. She was going to make him work for it. Steven couldn't help but be attracted to her high level of confidence, not to mention how mysterious she was.

Thinking about it a little longer, Steven decided to take Samantha's advice and find out from Joey how to get in touch with her. In order to do that, he would have to tell him that Samantha had told him that she was his niece. It didn't really matter, though, because Steven knew he wasn't going to be confrontational with Joey about it. He wasn't even going to ask him why he lied.

The sound of the door leading from the living room onto the balcony sliding open startled Steven. Amber, his favorite stripper from Joey's Bar, appeared. She was only partially clothed, but even that was more than he'd ever seen her wear at the bar. He had finally asked her to come home with him tonight, and she had gladly accepted the invitation.

"Hey Steven," she said to him, sitting in his lap and putting her arms around his neck. "Are you ready to come back inside now? I've been waiting on you."

Chapter 23

It was a little after two in the afternoon and John was eating a late lunch with Elizabeth Herrington at The Ivy, one of LA's most trendy restaurants. The two of them had become good friends over the past few weeks, having bonded since they both believed that Cameron was being wrongly suspected by the police and misrepresented by the media.

The media was relentlessly hounding the entire Herrington family, which is why Elizabeth was wearing a blonde wig to disguise herself. For her to even come to such a see-and-be-seen restaurant under these circumstances was a brave venture, but the way she was looking at it, it wasn't going to do her any good to sit at home feeling sorry for herself. She needed to get out and be around people.

The media didn't harass John as much as they did everyone else involved in all this drama. They knew that he was Harmon's live-in boyfriend, but they didn't pay much attention to him and certainly didn't follow him around in search of a story. That's why he didn't feel the need to disguise himself.

John's friendship with Elizabeth began when he called her a couple of weeks after Allison's funeral and asked her to meet him somewhere so that they could talk. He told her right then on the phone that he was certain that Cameron wasn't involved in Allison's death and that she was being falsely accused by the media and wrongly suspected by the police. She agreed to meet him at a Starbucks on Wilshire, where they talked for almost two hours about Cameron's situation.

John told Elizabeth that Harmon was completely convinced that Cameron was behind Allison's murder and wasn't even considering any other possibilities, despite the fact that Carter Greenfield seemed to be a shady character. John also told Elizabeth that Harmon was totally crazy, and would do absolutely anything, including lie to the police about Cameron, to make sure that Cameron went to prison. He vowed to Elizabeth at the Starbucks that he wasn't going to sit back and let Cameron go to prison for a crime she didn't commit without doing everything he could to help her prove her innocence. He explained to her that he didn't love Harmon anymore because she was such a cold-hearted woman, and that the only reason he was still with her was because he felt sorry for her, and didn't feel right about leaving her all alone to deal with the tragedy of her daughter's death. He told her that he was going to get out of the relationship as soon as Harmon had a little more time to grieve properly. With both of them now eating at The Ivy, John told Elizabeth that it was now time for him to end things with Harmon.

"I just can't take it anymore," he told her. "She's the most vindictive and evil person I've ever been around. I've never met anyone who even comes close to her."

Elizabeth didn't say anything. She only listened and nodded her head understandingly every now and then. On one hand, she was glad for John that he was getting out of such a bad relationship, but on the other hand, she kind of wished that he would stay with Harmon a little while longer so that he could be a spy for her and let her know what was going on between Harmon and the police. Sometimes she wondered if Peter knew more than he told her.

"I should have ended things with Harmon a long time ago. She's been treating me badly for a while now. All of this is nothing new. The reason I didn't end things before was because I really did love and care about her, and kept hoping she would change and we would be able to work things out. As soon as I realized that she wasn't ever going to change, Allison was killed, and like I already told you, I haven't had the heart to break up with her since then."

"John, you've done everything you can do," Elizabeth finally said, deciding to give her opinion. "You've been more than nice to Harmon, but she hasn't appreciated anything you've done for her. She's a wicked woman, and you're never going to be able to change that. Believe me when I say that you're doing the right thing by breaking up with her. You'll be much better off without her."

"Oh, I know that now," John said, taking another bite out of his hamburger. "I'm fully aware that she's trouble, and that I don't need to be involved with her."

"Then what are you worried about?" Elizabeth asked him, noticing that he seemed very anxious today.

"I'm worried about what she's going to do when I tell her I don't want to be with her anymore," he said, looking Elizabeth directly in the eyes. "I'm afraid she might try to kill me or something. You don't understand. She's always out for revenge, and doesn't stop until she gets it. I don't think anyone besides me knows just how crazy she really is."

As he said this, a wave of fear engulfed Elizabeth. She didn't want anything to happen to John. He was such a nice man. Was he right about Harmon? Surely she wasn't *that* crazy. Not wanting to think about it any longer, she steered the subject of their conversation back in the direction it had been taking before they were talking about Harmon.

"So you really think that Carter might have killed Allison?" she asked. John was a little taken aback by the abrupt change in conversation, but he didn't say anything about it. He understood that Elizabeth was more interested in clearing Cameron's name than giving him advice about Harmon.

"No, I didn't say that," he replied. "I just think it's definitely something that the police should look into more than they have. He seems unstable and obviously has a lot of problems."

Elizabeth took another bite of her food.

"It's obvious to me that he's guilty," she said. "Why else would he run like this?" Carter had been missing for almost twenty-four hours.

He'd disappeared when he found out the police were on the way to the beach house to question him again.

"The police don't know for sure that he's running. They only know that he hasn't been seen since yesterday afternoon. They've issued a state-wide search for him, though, so I'm sure he'll turn up soon."

"He's running," Elizabeth said. "I know he is. From what Cameron tells me, he hardly ever leaves the Malibu beach house except to go to the bars or to make a drug deal, so it's not like him to be gone for this long. That's how I know."

"You're probably right. From what I hear, he's nothing but trouble."

"They have to find him," Elizabeth said, her worry evident all over her face. "They just have to. If there's any chance that he's the person who killed Allison, then we have to be able to prove it so that Cameron will be able to move on with her life and not go down for a crime she didn't commit."

John could see Elizabeth's fierce determination in her eyes. He knew that she wasn't going to allow herself to rest until Cameron's name was cleared. He knew that even though Cameron hadn't been arrested yet, Elizabeth was still always a nervous wreck that she was about to be arrested because the police were constantly questioning her and trying to make a case against her. The media was also always following them around because the story was still a national news sensation. The news coverage was making Elizabeth even more of a nervous wreck about Cameron's predicament.

"Cameron's not going to go down for this," he said, trying to give her some assurance. "We're not going to let that happen. I'd be surprised if they ever even have enough on her to arrest her. The truth will eventually come out."

Elizabeth wiped a tear from her eye. "I sure hope so," she said. "Because Cameron's a good girl who just has too many problems right now. She's trying so hard to cope with Allison's death. Allison wasn't just her stepsister. She was her best friend too. To be accused of taking her life is really taking its toll on her. On top of that, she's pregnant. She doesn't deserve all this. It's too much for a nineteen-year-old to handle."

"I agree with you there," John said solemnly as his cell phone rang, interrupting their conversation. He looked to see who it was and was a little surprised to see that it was the caller. He hadn't called for a couple of days, so John had hoped that he had given up on torturing him. No such luck. John wasn't sure whether or not he should answer it in front of Elizabeth. He hadn't told her about the calls yet, and he didn't want her to worry about it.

His cell phone was still ringing.

"Go ahead and answer it," Elizabeth said, taking another bite of her food.

"Hello," John said, finally picking up.

"Hi, John. How have you been? It's been a while since we've talked. I've been busy the past couple of days and haven't had the chance to get in touch with you."

"I've been fine," John said, making sure he kept his answer short. He wasn't going to be friendly with this guy.

"Good, good," the caller said. "And are you and Elizabeth Herrington enjoying your little rendezvous at The Ivy? It's been a while since I've eaten there. Maybe I should join the two of you next time."

Chapter 24

Harmon was lying awake in her bed, mad as hell. She was slightly off the deep end right now, and she knew it. There was too much going on at one time, and it was all stressing her out and making her want to yell at someone.

The police in LA had been in touch with her off and on all day. They'd been asking her questions about where Carter Greenfield might have taken off to. She'd already told them probably half a dozen times that she didn't have any clue to his whereabouts, so she didn't know why they kept calling her. All she knew was that the kid was a complete and total screw-up. There was no telling where he was.

Harmon knew that since Steven was his best friend, *he* was who the police should be pestering. He claimed he didn't have any idea where Carter was, but Harmon wasn't so sure. She knew how close those two were and she had a feeling Steven might be covering for him. Ever since those boys were little kids, they had told each other everything, so why would that change now?

Harmon didn't really care whether or not Steven was covering for Carter. She didn't believe that Carter was Allison's killer, so why should she care? Harmon wished that the police wouldn't waste their time and resources on trying to find Carter when Cameron was who they should be taking into custody. There was no doubt in Harmon's mind that Cameron was responsible for Allison's murder. She didn't know whether or not Cameron was actually the one to fire the shots, but she knew that if she wasn't, then she hired whoever *did* fire them. Either way, the way Harmon looked at it, the girl deserved to spend the rest of her life locked behind bars, and she wasn't going to rest until that's exactly where she was.

It made Harmon furious to think about how jealous Cameron must have been of Allison all these years for her to do something like this. Allison had always been a little better than Cameron when it came to looks and popularity, and apparently it had been too much for Cameron to handle. Harmon had always felt like her daughter's friend had an inferiority complex, but she never suspected that it was this deep. Now that she knew, however, she couldn't really say that she was *that* surprised. After all, Cameron *was* the daughter of David Simms, the man who had always had the biggest inferiority complex of anyone Harmon knew. She found it funny that David, the poor little boy from the wrong side of the tracks, had worked all his life to overcome his past and heighten his place in the world, only to end up committing suicide. It went to show that everyone back in high school had been right about him. Some people just weren't meant to be a part of the elite crowd. Some people were born trash and never became anything better. Harmon now knew that David was one of those people. Even though she had still thought that she was better than David all these years, she had at least given him credit for achieving financial success by opening his own accounting firm. Now, she had no respect for him anymore, just like she hadn't when they were younger.

Harmon didn't think that Elizabeth was any better than David was. She had always loathed her and thought that she was socially beneath her. Elizabeth thought she was just as good as Harmon just because she lived in Beverly Hills too and was friends with a few famous people. Harmon begged to differ. Elizabeth was nothing but trash as far as she was concerned, even if she was married to Peter now. After all, she would have to be trash to have given birth to a creature as ruthless as Cameron.

Still lying in her bed, Harmon decided that she didn't want to dwell on Cameron and Elizabeth any more tonight. She was sick and tired of worrying about them and about getting justice for Allison. She knew she needed to just quit worrying, and sit back for a while and see what happened. Besides, she needed to look out for herself for a while. She'd been neglecting her own needs lately.

Harmon felt that her main need was to get Peter back. Not having him by her side during her time of grieving for Allison was the worst part about all this. Ever since this happened, she had realized just how much she actually *did* love and care for him. The amazing love they'd been able to provide for each other throughout their marriage was a once in a lifetime kind of love. What she had with John didn't even come close to what she'd had with Peter, and she was sure that Peter would say the same thing about his relationship with Elizabeth. She could tell that he was completely miserable with Elizabeth. Even though Elizabeth was young and beautiful, she didn't make him happy. She wasn't what he needed out of a marriage, so Harmon could only hope that their marriage fell apart soon. Well, she could do a little more than hope, and planned on doing so. She was going to do everything in her power to make sure that Peter left Elizabeth and came back to her.

Harmon's thoughts were interrupted by the ringing of her cell phone. She saw that it was Sonny calling. Sonny was her private investigator. She knew that he'd been following John around all morning trying to find out what he was up to. Harmon wasn't exactly sure yet what John was up to, but she did know that he had been very withdrawn from her lately and seemed to be avoiding her. She didn't care if their relationship ended, but she'd be damned if she was going to let him be the one to end it.

"Hello," she answered.

"John is having lunch with Elizabeth at The Ivy as we speak," the detective said. Harmon's face flushed with rage. So that's what he was up to, she realized. If he was going to cheat on her, couldn't he have at least chosen someone a little more respectable?

"Thanks for letting me know," she said through gritted teeth. As soon as she got off the phone with Sonny, she dialed Leonard Holt's number. She had heard enough about John. She knew what she had to do.

Chapter 25

Elizabeth didn't quite know how to deal with the stress of everything that was going on around her. Both Cameron and she were now showing and suffering from morning sickness almost every day. In addition to that, the police were still trying to pin Allison's murder on Cameron, which was causing Cameron so much worry that sometimes she could hardly function. Elizabeth was concerned that this was going to somehow negatively affect the health of the baby her daughter was carrying.

As if the fear of spending the rest of her life in prison wasn't enough stress for Cameron to deal with, she also had to deal with the invasiveness of the media. They hounded her on a daily basis. Throngs of reporters were camped out in front of their house at all times. The nightly news programs hardly discussed anything else but the Herrington murder, and the supermarket tabloids were trashing Cameron every week. Just yesterday, Cameron's lawyer told her that *Gossip Weekly*, one of the trashiest rags in print, had run a story on her. When Elizabeth went to a local supermarket to pick it up to read it, she felt nothing but rage welling within her when she saw the headline.

The words *Cameron's Murder-Suicide Gone Wrong* were screaming off the page at her. The story cited someone who said she was "a close friend of the Herrington family" as saying that Cameron had confessed to Elizabeth that she'd murdered Allison, and had planned on immediately killing herself after doing so because she was mad about Carter getting Allison pregnant with his child. The source then said that Cameron "chickened out" when it came time to turn the violence on herself

Elizabeth knew that this article was completely fabricated. She didn't for a second believe that anyone had given *Gossip Weekly* this information. One of their trashy writers just made it up. Elizabeth also knew that the lawyer she hired to represent Cameron was right. They were going to have to sue the tabloids if they wanted this slander to stop, so sue them was exactly what they were going to do.

Chapter 26

It had been three weeks since John left Harmon, and he was now all settled in at the condo he was renting in the Hollywood Hills. The condo was just off Benedict Canyon. John had been working on his screenplay a lot since he'd moved out of Harmon's place. He had a lot more time to work on it now that he didn't have to be with Harmon all the time. She'd been so high-maintenance, and required way too much attention…attention that he hadn't been willing to give her. Leaving her was going to prove to be the best thing he'd done since he'd changed his identity from Neil Hudson to John Parker. She wasn't bringing out the best in him. In fact, she was bringing him down. She was a bitter woman who wasn't happy unless she was making everyone around her as miserable as she was.

John knew that the reason Harmon was bitter was because her dreams for her life hadn't been realized. She'd wanted to continue her career as a teen actress into her adult years, but had failed in doing so. She'd also ultimately failed in her dream of being the wife of a wealthy man. She'd been the wife of a wealthy man for a while, but when he divorced her, he crushed her success at that. As crazy as it was, Harmon was now convinced that that she'd failed at making one of her kids into a star. As soon as Allison achieved a little success and got the lead role in *Deceptive Intentions*, she was murdered. Considering this,

John couldn't help but feel sorry for Harmon, even though she was totally crazy and mean as a snake. She was convinced that she was a total failure in life and the sad part about it was that John had to agree with her. He didn't think she was a failure for the same reasons that she did, though. He deemed her a failure because she had no sense of values, and had her priorities all out of order. Instead of focusing on family, friends and what matters most in life, she spent all her time trying to gain worldly success. She only became more miserable the longer that success eluded her.

It was now almost midnight, and John was relaxing in his living room. He'd fixed himself a drink and was thinking about all the crazy things that were going on around him lately. He found it ironic that he'd left his life as Neil Hudson to escape drama only to once again become involved in a situation consisting of a murder and a person being falsely accused of a crime. John knew that something really screwed up was going on here, and he wanted to unravel it because the Herrington family wasn't going to be safe until the vicious person responsible for Allison's murder was locked up. He also had to help out because he needed to help Cameron clear her name. His friendship with her and her mother had deepened even more lately and he felt like they needed his help.

John knew it would be easier on him to not get involved in this, but because he himself had once been in the same situation that Cameron was now facing, he felt an obligation to help her clear her name. Just a few years ago, it had been him who was falsely accused of murder, so he knew how it felt. The amount of pain it had caused him was immeasurable. Knowing that someone he knew was going through the same thing he'd gone through was almost too much for John to take. That's why he wanted to do everything in his power to help Cameron prove her innocence. He didn't want another innocent person to have to suffer the disgrace of being accused of a crime they didn't commit.

The media made John madder than the police did. Even though the police were barking up the wrong tree by trying to build a case against Cameron, at least they honestly thought they were making an effort to bring Allison's killer to justice. The media, on the other hand, weren't doing any such thing. All they were interested in doing was taking advantage of Allison's murder by sensationalizing it to provide entertainment for the public. The supermarket tabloids were the worst of all. John felt nothing but resentment towards them for the way they treated him after his family was killed. They wrote such horrible and false things about him, which helped turn the public against him. Now they were doing the same thing to Cameron. They were basically convicting her when charges hadn't even been brought against her.

John felt just as sorry for Elizabeth as he did for Cameron. He could only imagine how horrible it must be for her to see her daughter go through something like this. It would have been bad enough for Cameron to be falsely accused of murdering some random person, but the fact that she was being accused of murdering her stepsister made it so much worse. John knew just how much worse it actually did make it. He'd loved Kelly and his daughters more than he'd ever loved any other people before. Kelly was his one true soul mate, and he knew that no matter how hard he tried, he wouldn't be able to find another woman like her. There was no way that the connection he had shared with her could ever be duplicated. In addition to Kelly, Molly and Grace had been like angels sent to him from God. They'd brought such great joy to his life, and made him much happier than he had ever hoped to be. Being accused of viciously murdering the people he cared the most about almost crushed his will to live. He didn't want for Cameron and Elizabeth to want to die like he had wanted to.

The more John thought about everything, the more upset he became. This whole thing was so incredibly sad to him. As far as he knew, Cameron had never done anything that should have made anyone distrust her to the point of thinking that she was capable of killing someone. She didn't deserve to be treated like this. The whole thing was just a shame.

Not wanting to think about it anymore tonight, John turned on his TV hoping it would distract him from all of this. He needed to wind down before he went to bed.

Chapter 27

It was almost two in the morning and Steven was sitting in an inconspicuous parked rental car in the parking lot of Joey's Bar. He was smoking a cigarette. He'd been sitting here for over four hours keeping an eye out for Samantha Taylor. He'd rented the car from a dealership in Santa Monica because he knew that his red Mercedes convertible would stand out too much for what he was doing tonight. He needed to be incognito and this old brown Buick was perfect for the job.

Joey's was packed out since it was Friday night. The place was so crowded that people were even hanging out in the parking lot. Typical of Joey's clientele, most of the people appeared to be lower-class, so there was no way that he wouldn't spot Samantha if she was dressed as nice as she usually was. The girl stood out in a hole-in-the- wall place like this. There was no doubt about that.

Steven took a drag on his cigarette and wondered if it was sort of stupid for him to be going to all of this trouble to find Samantha when she'd told him to just ask Joey how to get in touch with her if he wanted to. The reason that Steven didn't just go ask Joey about her was because he didn't think that he would tell him anything. He'd already lied to him about her. Joey said that he had only seen her once and couldn't even remember her name, when according to Samantha, she was his niece. There was something shady as hell going on here, and Steven wanted to find out what it was. For some reason, Joey hadn't wanted him to know that Samantha was his niece and Steven didn't have any idea why. It didn't make sense unless Joey and Samantha were in cahoots, and were up to something. The way that she had popped in at Joey's twice while Steven was there and tried to seduce him without even getting to know him was weird. It was almost like he was being set up or something.

Steven finished his cigarette, then immediately lit another one. He couldn't believe that he was actually worrying about this Samantha girl at a time like this. Here he was staking out a bar in the Valley, when a guy wanted by the police for questioning regarding Allison's murder was hiding out in a secret room underneath his beach house. Steven knew that agreeing to harbor Carter at the beach house was a huge mistake because now if Carter was caught, Steven would be arrested as an accomplice. Steven felt like he didn't really have much of a choice when it came to helping Carter out, though, because his friend had been through so much and he felt sorry for him. It seemed like everyone who didn't believe that Cameron was guilty believed that Carter was the one that the police should be focusing their investigation on. Steven didn't know whether or not Cameron was innocent, but he did know that Carter was. He had full faith in his friend and knew that everyone who was accusing him was wrong. He didn't for a second believe that Carter had anything to do with his sister's death. It wasn't even a possibility. Carter wasn't evil enough to do something like that. He might have a lot of problems, but he didn't have a violent bone in his body.

Steven understood why some people believed that Carter was guilty, though. People had jumped to the conclusion that he'd been so mad at her for not wanting to have an abortion that he snapped and killed her. Carter's history with doing hard drugs didn't do anything to help his public image. Almost everyone who knew him already deemed him to be unstable because he'd had so many stints in rehab, so these people couldn't help but wonder if he was involved in Allison's murder.

Steven took another drag on his cigarette and inhaled the smoke deep into his lungs. He looked at his watch. It was now a little past two-thirty and Joey's was still crowded. He watched as a black limo pulled into the parking lot and came to a stop close to the door of the bar. Everyone in the parking lot was gawking. Nothing like this ever happened at Joey's.

Steven watched as the chauffeur got out of the limo and walked around the vehicle to open the door for its passenger. He was shocked when he saw who stepped out of the limo. It was Samantha Taylor, looking as gorgeous as ever.

Steven's cell phone rang. He didn't recognize the number that was calling him, so he ignored it until he noticed that Samantha was standing by the door to the bar with a cell phone to her ear. She was staring directly at him with a mischievous smile on her face.

"Hello," he answered, ducking down in the Buick, hoping the caller wasn't who he thought it was.

"Hi there sexy," Samantha Taylor said, her throaty voice already making him want her. "Are you just going to sit out here all night or are you going to join me inside?"

Chapter 28

Carter was sick and tired of being confined in one room. He was *way* too claustrophobic for this. He'd been in the secret room in the Herrington's beach house for two days now, and he knew it would probably be at least another month before he saw the light of day. If he wanted to get away with this and not get caught by the police, he was going to have to stay put and out of sight. Once the police quit pursuing him as heavily as they were now, and once the media attention surrounding Allison's murder and his disappearance died down, he was going to make a run for it. He was going to go out and make a fresh start somewhere new…as far away from LA as he could get. He was tired of California and all of the bullshit he had been through here. He wanted to have a normal life, maybe even get married and have kids. What he wanted most of all, though, was to get off drugs and stay off them. He knew that staying clean was the only way that he was going to make something of himself.

Carter knew that right now wasn't the appropriate time to deal with his drug problem, though. He was going to need all the coke and pills he could get to help him get through being confined like this. Thankfully, Steven knew how bad he needed drugs right now, so he'd been keeping him well supplied. There were lots of dealers here in Malibu.

Even though Carter hated being forced to hide out like this, he didn't have any regrets. He'd been forced to hide to avoid being arrested for Allison's murder. He couldn't go to prison for the rest of his life. His life so far had sucked, and he wasn't about to sit back and let his future get ruined too.

Carter thought about how he'd had nothing but problems over the years. His childhood and adolescence had been hell on earth. It seemed like so many kids avoided becoming friends with him because he was such a problem child and was always in serious trouble. Hardly any girls he dated during his teen years had stuck around for long. None of them wanted to get serious with him. They were all too afraid to. With his bad reputation, he didn't even have a chance of getting a nice girl, and a nice girl was what he wanted. All he'd ever wanted was to meet a good girl with who he could settle down and have a healthy relationship with. He'd never wanted to be the wild child he'd always been, but he just didn't know how to behave himself. He was one of those people who genuinely wanted to do right and stay out of trouble but really didn't know how to go about doing that.

The only girl who had ever really given him a chance was Allison Herrington. She hadn't cared about his wild ways and all the rumors connected with him. She truly loved him for who he was, and didn't pay any attention to the people who talked trash about him. Carter deeply regretted how badly he had screwed things up with Allison. Even though she was the only girl who would have a serious relationship with him, he'd treated her like shit and he felt horrible about it. He had never been physically abusive towards her, but he had been very verbally abusive. He had always tried to cut her down to make himself feel better about his own life. Carter's parents had committed suicide when he was twelve, and ever since then, he'd had low self-esteem. He always felt like everyone made fun of him for what his parents did and because he lived with his grandmother. Since he never talked with anyone about what his parents did, for years he pent up all of the rage he felt toward them. He'd unleashed that rage on Allison by being mean to her. She was the person he unleashed it on because she was the only person he ever got close to. Well, he had become *sort* of close to Steven over the years and definitely considered him to be his best friend, but he hadn't become close enough to him to reveal his true personality. He had never confided in Steven how much he hated his parents for killing themselves. He hadn't even discussed this with Allison. He'd only taken out all of his psychological problems on her.

Not wanting to think about his problems anymore, Carter curled up on the cot that Steven had given him and thought about happier times…his life with Allison before she was taken away from him…before she told him she was pregnant. He needed to get some sleep, and thinking about his life before all this happened was the only way that he was ever at peace enough to fall asleep.

Chapter 29

Steven was sitting at a table with Samantha Taylor in a small coffee shop a couple of blocks away from Joey's Bar. They were the only people in the place besides the people who worked there. Steven couldn't believe that he'd talked Samantha into coming here with him instead of going inside Joey's. She was playing so hard to get, he'd been afraid she wouldn't leave Joey's with him.

"So, why exactly did you lure me here?" Samantha asked him, batting her eyes and leaning forward as she sipped her coffee. "I hope you realize just how lucky you are that I came with you. I'm not normally a girl to be lured." Even though he knew Samantha was flirting with him, Steven didn't like the way she was talking down to him.

"First of all," he began. "I didn't lure you here or anywhere else for that matter. You've been the one who's been trying to lure *me*. And second of all, you're the lucky one. I don't ask just any girl to come hang out with me." Samantha smiled at him, still sipping her coffee.

"You're a confident guy," she said. "I like confidence in a guy. It lets me know that you know who you are and what you want out of life." She paused. "And so what if I *have* been the one doing the luring? Is there something wrong with that?"

Steven was becoming more and more interested in Samantha. She was beginning to open up and be more honest with him, which was a step in the right direction. He wanted to find out more about her, though. He still wondered if maybe he was being set up or something. It was really weird that Joey felt the need to hide the fact that she was his niece.

"No, there's nothing at all wrong with you showing some interest in me and trying to get to know me. I *do* think that there's something wrong with you acting so weird every time I run into you. You've approached me twice at Joey's, only to leave abruptly both times." Samantha was still smiling at him and seemed to be thoroughly enjoying the way their conversation was going.

"I'm a very mysterious girl, Steven," she cooed at him, clasping her hands in his on the table. "I have a lot of secrets…secrets that need to stay secrets."

"What kind of secrets?" Steven asked, trying to find out as much as he could while she was opening up to him. It wouldn't surprise him at all if she got up and walked out of the coffee shop at any time.

"Oh, you know," she said slyly. "Just secrets. Everyone has them. I'm sure you have a few yourself."

"My secrets don't interfere with my social life," Steven said. "When I begin a conversation with someone at a bar or a club, I typically stick around to finish it."

Samantha batted her eyes at him again.

"Well, I'm sticking around right now, aren't I?"

"Yeah, that's true," he acknowledged. "But you still haven't told me anything about yourself."

"What exactly is it that you want to know?"

"Let's start with where you're from."

"California born and raised," she said. "I grew up here in the Valley. What else do you want to know?"

"What do you do for a living?"

She laughed. "I'm afraid I can't tell you that, big boy."

"Why not?" Steven asked. "I don't think that should be too difficult of a question for you to answer, unless it's something shady."

She was still smiling at him. "Maybe it *is* shady," she said. "Why would that matter to you?" Steven could see that this wasn't going anywhere, so he changed the subject.

"Are you and your uncle close?" he asked, referring to Joey.

"I guess you could say that," she answered. "We weren't close at all when I was a kid but these past few years I've gotten to know him a lot better."

"Why weren't you close when you were a kid?"

"Family problems. My mother is Joey's sister. They had a falling out twenty years ago and haven't really had that much contact with each other since. No one ever told me what the falling out was about, though. My mom just never talked about Joey. I didn't even know she had a brother until I was twelve."

"So why are you and Joey spending time together now?"

"Oh, we don't really spend that much time with each other. I just go into his bar from time to time. That's how I met back up with him after all these years. I went into Joey's Bar with a couple of friends and recognized the owner as being the man who came over to the house for Christmas every three or four years. I thought it was pretty cool that I had an uncle that owned a bar. My mother is such a prude and always has been. She suffers from Catholic guilt. I always just assumed that her whole family was the same way."

Steven listened to what Samantha was saying, but realized that although hearing about her past was interesting, it wasn't really relevant to why she seemed to have such an interest in him. It also didn't explain why Samantha and Joey had gone to such great lengths to keep him from knowing that they were related. He decided to ask her about it. After all, he felt like he deserved an answer.

"Why did you and Joey not want me to know that you were related?"

Samantha suddenly became teary-eyed and looked away from him. Even though Steven had asked her this before, this time the question made her realize just how pitiful her life really was. Here she was, twenty-two-years-old with no future at all and hiding such a horrible secret.

"Because you're my last hope," she whispered to him, fighting back tears. Steven was now completely confused.

"What do you mean, I'm your last hope?" he asked her, his confusion evident by the tone of his voice. "Last hope for what? What are you talking about?"

"You're my last hope for redemption. Joey and I truly believe that you're the only person that can save me from this." She wasn't trying to hide her emotions at this point. Tears were streaming down her face.

Steven didn't know what to think.

"Save you from what, Samantha?"

"From becoming a victim like your sister did. I don't want to wind up like her."

Chapter 30

Harmon was sitting on the balcony of her mansion stewing about the way things were going. The detectives working on Allison's murder investigation still hadn't come up with enough evidence to arrest Cameron, and Harmon didn't for the life of her understand why. What more did they need? Cameron had a motive and as far as Harmon was concerned, anyone with half a brain should be able to see that she was guilty. Harmon knew that a lot of people did see it, though. Most of her friends saw it, and a lot of the news media saw it too. It was a shame the police didn't feel the same way.

It was also a shame to her that Peter didn't appear to be fully convinced of Cameron's guilt, either. He kept talking about Carter being on the run and saying that he was highly suspicious that the boy was behind Allison's death. Harmon didn't believe it for a second, though. There was no doubt in her mind that Cameron was responsible for this. She'd been jealous of Allison for years, and when Allison started dating Carter, it had been too much for her to handle. She'd snapped and done what she thought it was going to take to get Carter away from Allison. She'd killed her. The past couple of months anyone who saw Carter and Allison together could tell how completely and totally in love Carter was with her. He was infatuated with her, so Cameron thought the only way to get him to become interested in her was to get rid of Allison.

Even though the police were now spending more time investigating the possibility that Carter killed Allison, Harmon vowed to herself that she was going to eventually change this. She knew that even though it might take a while, she was going to make damn sure Cameron went down for this. She was nothing but a lying, murdering little bitch. She deserved to rot in hell for what she'd done to Allison. It wasn't Allison's fault that Cameron couldn't keep Carter around longer than the one night stand they'd had.

Harmon closed her eyes and tried to take her mind off Cameron. All of the anger she was harboring was beginning to get to her. She wanted to dwell on more pleasant thoughts, but instead her mind drifted to Peter. She sighed. Peter, the love of her life. What was she going to do about him? She wanted to get back with him more than anything else in the world, and she knew she wasn't going to be at peace until she was his wife again. Even though she felt so strongly about this, the sensible voice inside her head was telling her that getting back with Peter was a bad idea. Even though they both cared deeply for each other that didn't change the fact that they were toxic to each other. It had always been that way. From the very beginning of their long, rocky relationship, they'd brought out the worst in each other. Even though both Harmon and Peter were aware of this, neither one of them had sense enough to stay away from the other. Their love for each other had always been of a manic nature…more obsessive than anything else.

Harmon knew that it was completely crazy that her heart was telling her she needed Peter. Hell, just a couple of weeks ago she'd been in negotiations with a hit man to take his life, and now she wanted to walk down the aisle with him again. Although she felt this way, she also knew that if Peter didn't leave Elizabeth soon and come back to her, she was going to have to go through with having him killed. She wasn't going to have him killed to get revenge, though. Revenge wasn't it at all. Revenge hadn't been the reason she'd hired the hit man the first time. At the time, Harmon thought that she was trying to get revenge, but she now knew that wasn't it. She just wanted to make sure that Elizabeth wasn't going to get to have Peter if she couldn't. The same was true now. Peter was *her* man, not Elizabeth's. In Harmon's opinion, Elizabeth was nothing but a money-hungry little vulture who'd married Peter to advance her own financial situation.

It made Harmon almost physically sick every time she thought about Elizabeth being pregnant. Even if Peter did leave Elizabeth, they were still going to have to deal with the baby. As much as Harmon disliked this, there was nothing she could do about it. That was why she tried her best not to think about it. She was going to have to stop worrying about things that were beyond her control. Peter and Elizabeth's baby was probably always going to be in her life, and she was just going to have to accept it. Unless, of course, she got rid of Elizabeth and the baby…had them eliminated. Still sitting on her balcony, Harmon began to consider this option. The very thought caused her spirits to rise dramatically.

Chapter 31

John was sitting in the living room of his condo thinking about everything that had happened lately. He was beginning to feel guilty that he may have indirectly been the cause of Allison's demise. Even though the caller had told him that he wasn't behind Allison's death, John was having doubts. If the caller was crazy enough to kill Kelly and his daughters back in Atlanta, then there was no doubt that he wouldn't hesitate to kill again.

John was driving himself crazy trying to figure out who the caller was. He had no idea who could possibly have such a huge grudge against him. He couldn't for the life of him imagine why anyone would kill his family, and then still be tormenting him all these years later. John did know one thing, though, and that was that he was going to personally kill the son of a bitch when he found out who it was. There was no excuse for Kelly and the girls to have been robbed of their lives. As he thought about the family he lost, his heart melted just like it did every other time he allowed himself to think about them. Kelly, Molly, and Grace had been his everything. They were the lights of his life and he'd loved all three of them so much. He'd never forget the day he came home from Nashville after his Aunt Sarah had died to find all three of his loved ones dead in their beds with blood everywhere…each shot execution-style. No matter how hard he tried, John knew he would never be able to forget that horrifying day.

Six Years Prior

"I love you," Neil Hudson whispered to the eighty-year-old woman he'd always been so close to. She was lying in her hospital bed knowing that death was fast approaching. Aunt Sarah was his mother's sister. She'd always played a big part in his life, but after his parents died tragically when their house burned to the ground, John grew even closer to her. They were the only family each other had, so they stuck together. Seeing her close to losing her two-year-long battle with cancer was the hardest thing he'd had to deal with since his parents died.

"I love you too, Neil," Sarah said as she looked into his eyes. "And I'm real proud of the man you've turned out to be. I want you to know how proud of you your parents would be too."

Neil was doing everything he could to fight back tears, but was failing miserably. He didn't want to lose his Aunt Sarah. She'd always been so good to him. Even though he knew she was going to be fee from pain soon, it was still very hard for him to accept that this was happening.

"My parents would be very proud of you too," he said. "For always being there for me after they died. I was only twenty at the time… way too young to lose both parents. You made everything ok for me, though. You were determined I would make something of myself."

She smiled up at him.

"And it looks like I succeeded," she said. "Look at you. You've got a great job as an accountant, and you've got a beautiful wife and two wonderful daughters." Neil couldn't help but smile. Aunt Sarah was never one to be modest. She liked to brag on herself. Neil found it funny that she was taking full credit for his achievements.

After talking with his aunt a few minutes longer, he left the hospital and drove to her mansion in Brentwood, where he spent the night. The doctors told him that they were fairly confident that she would live through the night. That was the only reason he left his aunt's side. The doctors were right and Aunt Sarah fought her way through the night only to die at nine o'clock the next morning, just minutes after Neil was back at her side.

Neil then drove from Nashville to his home in Atlanta so that he could discuss funeral arrangements with Kelly. He found it odd that he wasn't able to get in touch with Kelly the whole drive home. It wasn't until he entered his oversized home in the Buckhead area of the city, though, that he realized that something was terribly wrong. The house was ransacked and one of the back living room windows was broken. Neil ran upstairs to make sure that everybody was okay, but in his gut he already had a good idea of what he was going to discover. His gut feeling didn't adequately prepare him for the horror that was awaiting him, however.

He found Kelly's body first. She was lying in the bed and looked peaceful, except for the fact that blood was all over the sheets and there was a big hole in the side of her head. It was obvious that someone had shot her while she was sleeping.

"Oh God, please help me," Neil cried out, not believing what he was seeing. "Please don't let this be happening." He rushed over to Kelly's body to see if she had a pulse. She didn't. Completely in shock, he then ran down the hall to Molly's room, where the same blood-drenched scene was waiting on him. Without even pausing, he then ran to Grace's room. The same thing…blood everywhere…his daughter's lifeless body. Everything was a blur.

Neil was screaming in horror at this point. He felt like he'd been hit by a train. His heart was pounding and his head was spinning. He rushed back to the master bedroom and called the police.

"You have to hurry," he yelled to the dispatcher. "My entire family's been murdered in their beds. I'm the only one left." He then clicked off the phone and knelt beside the bed, sobbing all over his wife's body until the police arrived.

Chapter 32

Elizabeth was held up inside of the house with Cameron. The place was still surrounded by media, and it was driving them both completely crazy.

"I just wish all these reporters would go away and leave us alone," Cameron sobbed, peeking out the kitchen window. "I don't understand why they're still hanging out here. It's been weeks since Allison was killed and I still haven't had charges brought against me."

Elizabeth was cooking spaghetti, irritated that Cameron wouldn't stop looking out the window every few minutes. She was trying so hard to make their lives as normal as possible, and constantly being reminded that their house was surrounded by the press didn't make her feel too good about her efforts.

"They're still out there because they're using Allison's murder to provide entertainment for the public," Elizabeth said bitterly to her daughter. "They're still hashing this case on all the nightly news shows."

"I know," Cameron said with a sigh. "It just seems like they would get bored with it."

"Get bored with it?" Elizabeth exclaimed. "I really hope you don't have any misguided ideas that the media is going to get bored with this any time soon. Allison was an actress and a very pretty one too. This story has grabbed the public's interest, and I have a feeling we are only at the beginning of this nightmare."

"What do you mean, Mom?" Cameron asked, still sobbing lightly and peeking out the window. She was so scared about how all of this was going to turn out. Her life was such a screwed-up mess. Here she was, nineteen, pregnant, and one of the prime suspects in what looked like was going to be one of the most famous murder cases in history. All she wanted to do was die. She had seriously considered following in her father's footsteps and committing suicide.

"I mean exactly what I said," Elizabeth said, trying to be patient with her daughter. She knew she shouldn't be ill with Cameron but it was hard to be in a good mood with anyone right now, considering what they were going through. "I think we're only at the beginning of this nightmare. I don't see the media leaving us alone any time soon."

Cameron was now sitting at the kitchen table watching her mother cook. "You're probably right," she said, wiping the tears from her eyes. "I'm just going to have to get over it and live my life and not let this drama get me down all the time."

"Everything's going to work out eventually, Cameron," Elizabeth assured her daughter. "I know it will. You're going to have a beautiful baby, and we're all going to be happy again soon."

"That's not enough, Mom. Having this baby isn't going to make me happy. You don't understand. I'm never going to be fully happy unless my name is cleared. Allison meant so much to me, and so many people think that I killed her. What I want more than anything in the world is to have my reputation salvaged. I want everyone to know how caring of a person I truly am."

Elizabeth continued to cook, but was beginning to tear up herself now. It pained her so much to hear Cameron describe how hurt she was by being falsely suspected by the police and media.

"I know you want people to know the truth," Elizabeth said. "But for right now, why don't you just be happy that you're not sitting in jail. If it wasn't for the lawyer Peter and I hired to represent you, you most likely would be."

"I'd almost rather be in jail than be free like I am with the whole world hating me."

"The whole world doesn't hate you," Elizabeth said. "I'm well aware of the fact that a lot of people think you're guilty, but a lot of people have changed their minds about you ever since Carter disappeared. A lot of people that did think that you killed Allison now believe that Carter killed her."

"He may *have* killed Allison," Cameron said thoughtfully.

"He very well may have," Elizabeth said. "I think that's a *very* good possibility. We all know that he was very much obsessed with her. He was furious with her for not agreeing to have an abortion."

Cameron slumped in her chair. She wished her mother would quit bringing up Carter. It made her too upset. He refused to have anything to do with her, and she didn't understand why. It wasn't like she wanted him to date her or something. She only wanted to be friends, and she only wanted that for the sake of the baby she was carrying. Cameron couldn't help but sometimes wonder if Carter believed that she was the one who killed Allison. That was the only reason she could come up with for why he didn't want to be friends with her.

Carter *had* told her, though, that he would play a big part in the baby's life. She knew he wasn't going to be a dead-beat dad. He was going to be there financially for the baby, as well as emotionally. Cameron's thoughts were interrupted by her mother, who was still hovering over the stove cooking spaghetti.

"Dinner's almost ready," she said, looking at her watch. "I sure hope Peter gets home soon. I hope he didn't end up having to work late." Cameron only nodded at Elizabeth and continued to stare into space. She was thinking about how wild the reporters outside would go once Peter's car pulled up outside. Anytime a member of the Herrington family came and went from the house, it was reported on every news station around the world. Cameron didn't understand why the media loved it that her mom was married to Peter Herrington, Allison's father. What difference did that make? Why did they get satisfaction dubbing the case "*A family Divided.*" She was beginning to wonder if all that these reporters wanted was a juicy story. Was there no one out there who wanted to get justice for Allison?

Her thoughts were interrupted by the sound of a car arriving in the driveway followed by the slamming of a door and reporters shouting. Elizabeth, closely followed by her daughter, ran to the front door to let Peter in. Elizabeth opened the door and stepped outside to greet her husband. She wanted the media to know that the family was still unified. Cameron stayed inside the front entrance hall listening to what was going on outside. What she heard next was the last thing she expected to hear. A gunshot…followed by screams of terror from the people gathered on the street in front of her house. They couldn't hold back their cries at what they saw. Elizabeth was lying motionless in a puddle of her own blood right in front of Peter's Porsche.

Chapter 33

Peter was sitting in the waiting room at Cedars-Sinai Medical Center, completely furious. Cameron was sitting with him listening to him rant. She wasn't saying very much, however. She was more worried about her mother and the baby her mother was carrying than she was angry about what had happened. Elizabeth was in emergency surgery right now. The doctors were fairly confident that she was going to be okay, but weren't certain about the baby.

"I can't believe that someone would do something like this to a pregnant woman," Peter fumed through gritted teeth. "With as much as we've gone through with Allison's death, to have this happen is completely unbelievable."

He got up from his chair and paced around the waiting room, which was empty except for the three of them. "If I ever get my hands on the son of a bitch who did this, I'll kill him," he raged. "No one's going to mess with my family like this. I just lost one child and now I might be about to lose another one. I'll be damned if I'm going to let whoever's behind this get away with it."

"I definitely think you're right when you say that you think whoever killed Allison is the same person who did this to Elizabeth,"

Cameron said, referencing the conversation they'd had a few minutes ago. "It would be too big of a coincidence for it to be someone else."

Although Cameron was devastated that this had happened to her mother, she was thankful that at least now the police might be able to see that she wasn't the person who killed Allison. Cameron had an airtight alibi this time, so there was no way the police could pin this on her. She was inside the house when the gun was fired.

"You're damn right it's the same person," Peter yelled, punching the wall. Cameron was a little surprised by how violent he was acting. "I never really believed it was you who killed Allison. I mean, I suspected you a little at first just because I couldn't figure out what was going on, but I never truly believed it. Harmon's the one who thinks that. I told her a long time ago that the detectives shouldn't be focusing their investigation solely on you."

Cameron was glad to hear that Peter didn't suspect her but was a little offended to know that he had suspected her at first. It amazed her how many people doubted her these days. What had she ever done so terrible that would make people believe she was capable of committing murder? She'd always been a good girl, unlike all of her wild friends. She'd always been the one in the group to keep her senses about her and a good head on her shoulders. She'd never been a drinker or a big partier. Sure, she was around it when she hung out with her friends, but she didn't participate in it.

Allison, on the other hand, was always getting into some sort of trouble. She was a wild child, and Cameron had often wondered if she would ever be tamed. Peter and Harmon had pulled their hair out with her ever since she was a little girl. She was a discipline problem throughout her childhood, and things only got worse in her teenage years. She'd started drinking at thirteen and was experimenting with drugs by the time she was fifteen.

Cameron would never forget the time a couple of years ago that Harmon caught her getting high with a thirty-five-year-old married rock star at the Herrington's East Hampton house. Harmon was so furious with her that she'd threatened to send her off to boarding school if she didn't straighten herself out. It was the last straw in a string of out-of-control events, one of which involved Allison crashing her brand new BMW Convertible into a tree in the Hollywood Hills while driving home from one of the popular crowd's wild parties.

When she realized that her mother was dead serious about sending her off to boarding school, Allison got her act together and had stayed out of trouble for the last two years. She'd thrown all of the energy she once used to be rebellious into developing her career as an actress. She took several acting classes in both New York and LA during that time and even did several commercials. Just a few months ago, she'd landed the role in *Deceptive Intentions*, which was highly anticipated to be the springboard for her rise to stardom.

Cameron knew she shouldn't be letting her mind wander like this when her mom was in surgery. She should be praying for a positive outcome and providing moral support for her Peter, who she knew was devastated by everything that had happened lately. Cameron was well aware that Peter had been through so much the past couple of months. From having to come to terms with his daughter's death, to having to deal with the fact his stepdaughter was suspected of killing his daughter. It was more than most people would have been able to handle emotionally.

A young doctor who appeared to be in his late twenties suddenly walked into the waiting room. Peter and Cameron looked at him, anxiously wondering whether he was bringing good news or bad news.

"Are you Peter Herrington?" he asked, walking over to Peter. The faint smile on the doctor's face allowed the family to breathe a sigh of relief.

"I am," Peter said, jumping up. "How are Elizabeth and the baby? Are they going to be okay?"

"Your wife is a very lucky woman," the doctor said. "The surgery went well, and both she and her baby are going to be just fine."

Chapter 34

John was speeding towards Cedars-Sinai Medical Center in complete and total disbelief. He'd first heard the news about Elizabeth being shot about an hour before. He'd been working out when the radio station he was listening to interrupted the music they were playing so that they could give their listeners the latest news about the Herrington saga. John was floored that someone would be so bold as to shoot Elizabeth in front of her house with as many people around as there were. The media was literally crawling all over the place with their cameras when it happened. John couldn't for the life of him come up with a reason why anyone would be so desperate to get rid of Elizabeth. Sure, he didn't know that much about her but everything he did know was good. She definitely wasn't the gold digging troublemaker Harmon made her out to be.

Harmon. Surely she's not responsible for this, he thought to himself. He definitely wouldn't put it past her.

His cell phone rang.

Private call.

"Damn," he yelled, slamming his fist on the steering wheel in anger. With everything that was going on, the caller was the last person he wanted to hear from right now.

"What do you want?" he answered, totally exasperated.

"Oh, just to check in and see what you're up to," the caller said with a chuckle. "You know me…always checking in with you these days."

John was trying very hard to control his anger, but couldn't help himself.

"Yeah, that's the one thing I can count on you to do," John said sarcastically. "Call and check in on me. You never seem to forget about me."

"You always crack me up, John," he said. "Always the funny one you are.

"What are you really calling me for this time?" John asked, knowing the call was probably pointless just like all this guy's other calls were.

"I really was just calling to say hi," he said. "And to find out what you think about this little ordeal with Elizabeth Herrington. It's so tragic, don't you think?"

John could feel his blood go cold. Surely the caller wasn't the person behind Elizabeth's shooting. John felt that if he was, then he himself was indirectly the cause of it. The thought really upset him. This guy had already hurt him so much when he killed Kelly and the girls, and John didn't want it to happen all over again now that he'd begun this new life.

"Did you have something to do with what happened to Elizabeth?" he asked the caller, dreading his answer.

"Absolutely not," the caller answered, genuinely sounding surprised that John would think that. "I'd never do something like this. What kind of person do you think I am?"

"The kind that killed my innocent wife and daughters." John heard his voice crack as he said this, but he managed to maintain control of himself.

"True, true," the caller said. "You've got a good point there, John. I definitely see where you're coming from. Most people who kill would do it again. Not me, though. Kelly and your daughters was a onetime thing." He paused. "Well, not a onetime thing," he clarified. "There *are* a few other people I'd like to kill, like *you*, of course."

"Why did you kill them?" John asked, keeping his voice cold even though he felt like his heart was being ripped out of his chest. "Why did you kill my family?"

"I've already told you, my friend. Because I'm jealous of you. You've always had more than me…always…for years it's been that way. You had a beautiful wife and two beautiful daughters. You didn't deserve them, though, so I had to take them away from you."

John was red with rage now. He couldn't believe what he was hearing, even though he already knew from previous telephone conversations with the caller that jealousy had a lot to do with why he'd killed his family.

"Who the hell are you?' John yelled into the phone, slamming on his brakes to avoid hitting the car in front of him, which had stopped abruptly at a red light on La Cienega. "And what do you mean I've had more than you for years? Have you even known me for years?" His whole body was shaking, he was so angry.

"Oh yes, John," the caller said, his voice now sounding completely evil. "I've always known you. I've always been there right with you, lurking in the shadows. You've just never noticed me."

"You're a son of a bitch," John yelled. "When I figure out who you are, I'm going to have you thrown in jai for the rest of your miserable life."

"You're never going to figure out who I am, John. I can promise you that. Do you want to know how I'm so positive of that? Because I'm not going to reveal myself to you until I decide the time is right to kill you."

Chapter 35

Harmon was in the master bedroom of her East Hampton mansion unpacking the four Louis Vuitton suitcases she brought with her. When she saw on the news that Elizabeth had been shot, she'd caught the first flight to New York. With all of the craziness going on in LA, she had wanted to get out of town for a while. What better place to run to than the Hamptons?

Harmon had always loved the Hamptons. When she was in her teenage years, her parents allowed her to spend most of her summers with her mother's sister, Louise, who owned a big house in Montauk. Those summers were the happiest memories she had of her childhood. She loved just getting away from the hustle and bustle of her acting career in LA to come out here, relax, and be a normal kid. Well, as normal as a kid who summers in the Hamptons can be.

As she grew older, Harmon still loved the Hamptons just as much as she did when she was little. Throughout the years, she'd made countless trips there. When Steven and Allison were little, she took them to the East Hampton house to spend most of their summers. They'd both loved it just as much as she did and spent hours playing on the beaches.

Harmon was still unpacking her suitcases but the fond memories of Allison made her stop and lie down on the bed to rest for a while. As she lay there, she thought about how much she missed her daughter and recalled all of the many fun times they'd shared together. Throughout these last two years, they'd grown especially close as Allison pursued a career in acting. Because Harmon was a former child television star, she gave Allison a lot of advice about the entertainment industry and paid for all of her acting classes.

Ever since Allison had entered her teen years, Harmon had pushed her to become an actress and had been thrilled when Allison finally came around and embraced the idea a couple of years ago. She was such a talented girl and Harmon knew that if she had lived she would have become a huge star.

Still lying in her bed, Harmon thought about how unfair it was that Allison's life had ended the way it had. No one deserved to be gunned down like that, especially in their own home. Home was the place where people were supposed to feel the safest.

Harmon was still totally convinced that Cameron Simms was behind Allison's death. She wasn't sure if Cameron was actually the one who pulled the trigger, but knew that if she wasn't, then she had hired it done. Every time Harmon thought about Cameron, she became raging mad. Her anger towards her overshadowed her grief for Allison by a long shot. She hated Cameron Simms more than she had ever hated anyone in her life and wasn't going to stop until Allison was either in prison or dead. One way or the other, she was going to get her back for what she'd done. If the police didn't get something on her soon, Harmon was going to have her eliminated.

Harmon was becoming more frustrated with the police every day. It seemed to her like they were just poking around on this case not even trying to make progress. For some reason, they still hadn't arrested Cameron when it was obvious that she was behind the murder. Harmon didn't know how much more clear it could be. The little tramp was pregnant by the father of the baby that Allison was carrying. She had the perfect motive. Harmon was convinced that Cameron killed Allison so that she could get Carter to fall in love with her.

"She wasn't going to sit back and let the father of her child's baby be with another girl," Harmon said aloud. "She wanted him all to herself."

A knock at the bedroom door made her jump.

"Come in," she called out. She watched as Anna, the elderly housekeeper who lived in the house full time, walked into the room.

"Mrs. Herrington," she said timidly, focusing her eyes on the floor. She had always been intimidated by Harmon because she never knew what kind of mood she would be in.

"Yes dear," Harmon said politely, which surprised Anna. Her boss had been in a bad mood just a few hours ago when she picked her up from the airport.

"There are two policemen waiting downstairs to see you."

Chapter 36

John had shown up at Cedars-Sinai Medical Center just after Peter and Cameron found out that Elizabeth and her baby were going to be fine. After they all visited with Elizabeth for a few hours in her hospital room, Peter went back home to get some rest while Cameron and John stayed with Elizabeth. Although she was still feeling weak from what had happened, she agreed to talk with them about everything that was going on with Allison's murder investigation.

John was now sitting by Elizabeth's bed with Cameron, not believing what the girl was telling him. What the hell was Harmon thinking?

"You mean to tell me that she took off to the Hamptons in the middle of Allison's murder investigation?" he exclaimed again, shaking his head in disgust. He couldn't believe how selfish she was. The police needed her here in LA in case something came up with the investigation that they might need her help with, yet she was off doing whatever she wanted to do in the Hamptons. It didn't make any sense. John knew that no normal mother would have left town with everything that was going on.

Elizabeth was shaking her head in disbelief too.

"Harmon is just in her own little world," she said. "Ever since I've known her, she's always done exactly what she wanted to do without giving any regard to other people."

John nodded in agreement.

"Believe me, I know," he said. "I lived with her for over a year."

"Yeah, I guess you and Peter know her better than anyone else does."

"Yeah, and I'm still surprised that she left town that fast without telling anyone. That's a little selfish even for Harmon. It's almost like she's running from something."

"That's what I told Peter," Elizabeth said. "It doesn't make any sense."

"What's Peter saying about it?"

"He thinks it's crazy and says he's going to call her back and tell her so later today. He was still too worried about me when she called to argue with her."

"So she just called him to tell him where she was?" John asked.

"Yeah, she called him as soon as her place landed in New York."

Cameron finally broke her silence.

"Mom, I've been giving it a lot of thought," she said casually. "And I'm seriously considering calling Harmon."

Elizabeth and John couldn't believe what they were hearing.

"What in the world do you want to call her for?" asked Elizabeth, her voice incredulous.

"Yeah," John echoed. "She's the one trying to have you thrown in jail."

"I just think it might do some good for me to talk to her directly about what happened to Allison. Maybe I can talk some sense into her and get her to see that I'm not the person behind the murder."

Elizabeth shook her head.

"No, Cameron," she said. "Harmon's already made up her mind and she's not going to change it at this point. She's completely and totally convinced that you're guilty."

"Yeah," John said in agreement with Elizabeth. "You need to stay as far away from that woman as you can get. She's crazy as hell."

Cameron suddenly started to tear up.

"So you're telling me there's nothing I can do or say that will ever change her mind? She's just always going to think I'm a horrible person?"

"Look Cameron," Elizabeth said sympathetically. "I know this is hard for you to accept, but right now a whole lot of people think that you're guilty of killing Allison. Harmon is one of those people and there's no telling what she'd do if you called her. She would probably call the police and tell them all kind of lies about what you said when you called her."

"I've never done anything so bad in my life that should make people believe I'm capable of committing murder," Cameron said, sobbing hysterically now. "I've always tried to live a good life and be a good person. I don't understand why people don't seem to care what I'm going through right now. I mean look at me, I'm nineteen and pregnant, and I've just lost my stepsister and now someone just tried to kill my mother." Tears streamed down her face.

John sat beside the bed silently observing this pitiful mother-daughter conversation. His heart was aching for Cameron, who was way too young to have all of these problems. He could see that the girl was on the edge of a nervous breakdown just like he had been when he was on trial for the murder of his wife and daughters. He wanted desperately to do something to help her but had no idea what that would be.

"I know how hard this has been for you," Elizabeth said, still embracing Cameron. "But I'm here for you. I've been here for you from the very beginning and I will continue to be here for you. You're not alone."

"Your mother's right," John chimed in. "I'm here for you too. Don't ever think you're in this thing alone."

A knock at the hospital room door interrupted their conversation.

"I wonder who that could be," Elizabeth said, hoping it wasn't a reporter. Peter had told her the hospital was surrounded by the media, so she wouldn't be surprised if one had somehow slipped inside.

"I'll get it," John said as he jumped up from his chair and made his way to the door. He opened it just a crack to see who it was. Four uniformed police officers were standing in the hallway.

"Is Cameron Simms here?" one of the men asked, moving closer to the door.

"Yes she is," John answered with a sinking feeling in his stomach. He thought he knew what was going on here. "May I ask what you need to see her about?"

Cameron walked up behind John and opened the door wider.

"What's going on, John?" Cameron asked, staring at the police officers. There was fear in her eyes.

"Are you Cameron Simms?" the same officer who spoke before asked.

"Yes, I am."

The officer pushed John out of the way and stepped inside the foyer. He then grabbed Cameron's hands and handcuffed her. "Miss Simms, you're under arrest for the murder of your stepsister, Allison Herrington. You have the right to remain silent when questioned. Anything you say or do may be used against you in a court of law. You have the right to consult an attorney…"

Chapter 37

Steven was relaxing in the TV room at the beach house and didn't know what to think. He was more confused than ever about what was going on in his life. He'd been held up in the house for days on end. The reason he didn't leave was because he didn't want to go anywhere. He wanted to just stay at home and try to piece this puzzle together. The only person he'd talked to in days was Carter, who was still hiding out in the secret room below the house, high as a kite.

Unlike Carter, Steven wasn't doing any drugs. He was staying clean so that he would be able to think logically about everything that had happened. He was hoping that maybe if he thought long enough, he would realize something that he hadn't realized before…that something would come to light.

He couldn't believe that Cameron had been arrested for Allison's murder. He thought for sure that the police believed Carter was the killer. All of the detectives' questions the last time he talked to them had something to do with Carter. Although Steven knew that the police had originally focused Allison's murder investigation on Cameron, he thought they'd changed their minds about her. The fact they hadn't and that she was sitting in a jail cell right now made Steven feel terrible. He really didn't believe Cameron was capable of doing something this horrible. She'd always been such a nice girl and a great friend to Allison. In his heart, Steven knew she wasn't guilty and desperately wished there was something he could do to help her. She was too nice of a person to be going through what she was going through.

Steven knew it must be terrible that on top of being arrested on murder charges, Cameron was pregnant with Carter's baby. As if all that wasn't enough, someone had also just tried to kill her mother. Steven also knew that with everything else that had happened, it was very likely that Cameron would have been sent over the edge if Elizabeth had been killed. There was only so much a person could handle and he felt that she had to be fairly close to the breaking point. Even though Steven wasn't really into the whole family thing, he really did wish that things would get better for his stepsister. It was high time a lucky break came her way. He believed that if the police could find out who *really* killed Allison, Cameron would be able to salvage her life and get it together.

What Steven wished more than anything right now was that his mother would lay off Cameron. He didn't understand how she could be so completely and totally convinced that she was guilty. She didn't even really know her that well. Although Allison and Cameron had been best friends since elementary school…long before they became stepsisters…Harmon had never made much of an effort to get to know her. She'd always thought Allison was too good to be friends with Cameron and at first had hoped they would outgrow each other. She wanted for Allison to be playmates with the children of the movie stars and the super-rich, and the Simms family didn't quite fit that bill. Even though they had money, they weren't as wealthy as the people Harmon liked to associate herself with. They weren't in show business either.

Steven just wished that his mother could be open to the possibility that someone besides Cameron could have murdered Allison. It didn't make sense for her to completely focus on Cameron when all of the evidence against her was circumstantial. His mother was so quick to judge and form opinions about people. This had always bothered him. She had a know-it-all attitude, but Steven had discovered that more often than not, she was wrong about things. Her many opinions and beliefs about people were often jaded and not based on fact. He saw his mother for the materialistic and stuck-up person that she was. He knew that money, fame, and social status meant everything to her. She didn't value the things in life that really mattered, such as family and true friendships. She was only focused on the superficial. He wished he could somehow change her attitude on life and make her see how wrong she was about everything.

Steven knew how rude his mother had always been to Elizabeth. Even before she'd married Peter, Harmon had looked down on her and refused to be friends with her despite the fact that their daughters were best friends. She'd always thought she was much better than her. Steven knew that his mother's intense scorn for Elizabeth and Cameron was the main reason she believed that Cameron was behind Allison's death. She'd had such a low opinion of them for so long that she'd convinced herself that Cameron was a lowlife capable of murder. Steven knew that his mother most likely didn't know anything about the evidence in Allison's case, so it wasn't as if she carefully examined the evidence before coming to the conclusion that Cameron was guilty.

Steven was aware that there really wasn't any concrete evidence pointing towards Cameron. That was why he wished his mother would lay off the police and quit putting pressure on them to build a case against Cameron. He knew that if she would just sit back and let the proper authorities do their jobs, they would have a lot better chance of finding out who was really behind Allison's murder. The police didn't need to be distracted by the raging-mad mother of a victim who was hell bent on making sure a specific person went down for this crime. Steven just wished he could convince his mother of that.

Chapter 38

Elizabeth was going completely crazy with worry inside of her room at Cedars-Sinai. Peter was sitting in the chair beside her bed trying his best to calm her but to no avail. She was all worked up over Cameron's arrest and refused to do anything but talk about their options concerning the situation.

"Rusty's a really good lawyer," she said, referring to Rusty Adams, the attorney they'd hired a few weeks ago. "But I don't know if he has what it takes to handle a case this big. I wonder if we should start looking for someone else to represent her."

"I don't know what you're talking about, Elizabeth," Peter said with a sigh. "How many times do I have to tell you? Rusty's one of the best lawyers in LA. He works for one of the most prestigious laws firms in the United States." He paused for a moment and then continued. "Besides, I have no idea what you're so worried about anyway. All of the evidence they have against her is circumstantial. I don't think there's any way a jury will convict her. Right now, unless there's something we don't know about, the prosecution doesn't have much of a case."

"Well, they've arrested her and are charging her for some reason," Elizabeth snapped at him. "They obviously think they have a case." She was sick and tired of him telling her she was overanalyzing things and that there wasn't anything for her to worry about. Cameron was sitting in a Los Angeles County Jail cell waiting to be charged with murder. It seemed to Elizabeth that maybe it was time to start worrying.

Elizabeth noticed that Peter seemed a little taken aback that she'd snapped at him. He had a hurt expression on his face, which made her want to yell at him even more. She felt that he just needed to toughen up, get with the program, and acknowledge the seriousness of their situation. Didn't he realize that there was good reason for her to be in panic mode?

"I'm only trying to help you stop worrying," Peter said, defending himself. "What do you want for me to do? Sit back and have a pity party with you? We both know good and well that that won't do any good."

"Listen here, Peter," she said, propping herself up on her pillow. "I didn't say anything about having a pity party. I'm not trying to be negative. I'm only trying to be realistic. Cameron is in a hell of a mess. There's no other way to describe it."

"We need to stop arguing," Peter said. "Arguing isn't going to do us any good either."

"You're right," Elizabeth agreed. "We need to be using this time to talk strategy. I wish Rusty was here right now."

"I already talked with him on the phone just a few minutes ago on my way here. Right now, he's focusing on posting bail. He wants to get Cameron out of jail as soon as possible. That's currently his number one priority."

Elizabeth nodded her head with approval, anxiety once again attacking her mind and soul. The thought of poor, helpless Cameron lying in a prison cell was almost too much for her to mentally handle right now. She was so worried about her daughter and hoped and prayed that she was okay. She didn't want for her to be scared or depressed. She prayed that Cameron was being optimistic and not giving up hope. She was only nineteen-years-old. She had so much to live for. Elizabeth only hoped that Cameron realized this and wasn't dwelling on negative thoughts. She'd talked to her once on the phone when Cameron got her one phone call from the jail and she seemed to be okay, although Elizabeth couldn't tell for sure. Cameron somehow managed to maintain her composure and not cry, but she was still low-key about everything.

Elizabeth was also tremendously worried about Cameron being in jail while pregnant. She knew that jail was no place for a pregnant girl to be. She was aware that anything and everything happened in jails. She'd heard the horror stories. What if someone beat her up and the baby was hurt? What if Cameron got too upset about things and this caused her to miscarry? What would happen then? Elizabeth knew exactly what would happen. Cameron would spend the rest of her life feeling guilty about it and would probably never get over it.

"How soon do you think we'll be able to get her out?" she asked Peter.

"Pretty soon," he said. "Rusty thinks it will be within the next day or two."

"That's good," Elizabeth said, suddenly feeling tired. She was still extremely weak from being shot and then having surgery. What she needed more than anything else was to get some rest but with all the panic-stricken thoughts racing through her head, that wasn't really a possibility. Elizabeth wished she could block it all out and relax, but she just couldn't.

Thoughts of Harmon were now making her start to worry. Elizabeth knew that Harmon had done nothing but try to convince both the police and the news media that Cameron had murdered Allison. She'd been doing this since the night Allison was found dead. She'd trashed Cameron's name all over the town. It made Elizabeth almost sick to her stomach when she thought about it. It upset her even more that as soon as Cameron was about to be arrested, Harmon took off to the Hamptons as if she was celebrating.

"Have you heard from Harmon?" Elizabeth asked Peter, who was still sitting in the chair beside her bed. She immediately knew something was wrong because all of a sudden he became very fidgety and looked real nervous when she mentioned Harmon.

"What is it? Elizabeth asked, suddenly getting very nervous herself. "Peter, what's wrong?"

"It's Harmon," he answered her. "The police think she had something to do with you being shot."

Chapter 39

Harmon was standing in the front entrance hall of her house not knowing exactly how to conduct herself. The two detectives in front of her were not from New York. They were from Los Angeles, which was why she was worried. They came all the way from California just to talk to her. That meant that something was up.

"How can I help you men today?" she asked, flashing them a smile. She was trying to be friendly and not let her nervousness show. Neither of the two men smiled back at her.

"We're here to ask you some questions about Elizabeth Herrington," one of them spoke up, closely watching her reaction. She visibly became even more anxious.

"Sure," she said, her voice shaky. "Why don't we go into the living room and take a seat. We'll be more comfortable in there." Harmon walked across the front entrance hall into the large living room with the two detectives trailing closely behind her. She took a seat on the sofa and motioned for them to sit in the chairs across from her. She'd regained her composure and was now presenting herself with more confidence. She realized that if she was going to get these two guys off her back, she was going to have to make a good impression on them. If she didn't, she knew they would just keep bothering her.

"I think it's absolutely terrible about Elizabeth," she said, shaking her head solemnly. "Absolutely terrible. I mean, who would do something so terrible as to shoot a woman with child?"

This time the other detective spoke.

"It is a terrible, terrible thing," he said, nodding in agreement. "That's why we're doing everything in our power to get to the bottom of it and find out who's responsible."

"I personally believe that the person who did this is the same person who killed my daughter." Harmon said. "I don't think there's any way that this could just be a coincidence."

Both detectives nodded.

"You may very well be right," one of them answered. "We're currently considering all possibilities."

The other detective took over at this point.

"Ms. Herrington," he began. "I understand that Elizabeth Herrington is married to your ex-husband."

"That's correct. Peter and Elizabeth have been married for a little over a year now."

"You've known Elizabeth for years, though, right?"

"Yes, my daughter, Allison, and her daughter, Cameron, became friends in elementary school and were best friends until the time of Allison's death." She paused. "Or at least it seemed as though they were best friends." She suddenly became a little nervous once again. She hoped she wasn't talking too much and appearing too eager to please them.

The detective didn't pause in his questioning.

"After reviewing the interviews that you've given detectives these past few weeks, I've gathered that you believe that Cameron is responsible for your daughter's murder?"

Harmon nodded.

"I have no doubt that that's the case," she said. "I am absolutely certain that Cameron is guilty. I heard she's been arrested, so apparently I haven't been too far off in my assumptions."

The detective didn't acknowledge Harmon's comment regarding Cameron's arrest. He had no desire to make extra conversation with her.

"Now that we've established how you feel about Cameron, I want to talk about how you feel about Elizabeth. What's your relationship with her like? Do the two of you get along?"

Harmon hesitated before answering him. She didn't want to lie, although she knew the truth would make her look bad. Because she didn't want for them to view her in anymore of a bad light than they already did, she decided to lie.

"Yeah, we get along great and always have."

"So you weren't mad when she married your ex-husband last year? There weren't any feelings of animosity?"

Harmon decided to be a little more truthful regarding these questions.

"I wouldn't say there was any animosity," she said delicately. "But I wouldn't say that I was exactly happy about Peter and Elizabeth getting married either."

"Why weren't you happy about it?" he asked. "You and Peter are divorced. Why would you care whether or not he remarried?"

"Well, we hadn't even been divorced two months before he started dating Elizabeth," Harmon explained, choosing her words carefully. "I think he moved a little fast, which made things harder on Allison and my son, Steven. They were just getting used to the idea that their parents were no longer together when Peter just all of a sudden brought a new love interest into the picture."

"I see," the detective said. "So your only reservation about Peter and Elizabeth's marriage was the effect the union would have on your kids?"

Harmon nodded.

"That's correct," she said. "I like Elizabeth a whole lot. She's a great person. My only concern was for Allison and Steven." Harmon was lying through her teeth, but she felt like that was her only option. She wasn't about to sit here and spill her guts to them about how she was still madly in love with Peter and hated Elizabeth for marrying him. If she did that, they would be convinced that she was behind Elizabeth's attack.

Even though Harmon thought she sounded convincing, she could tell the detectives knew she was lying. She didn't really care, though, because there was no way they could prove her true feelings towards Elizabeth. Harmon realized that she was going to have to be careful from this point forward. She was going to have to make sure that she didn't slip up and reveal her hatred of Elizabeth. She knew that these detectives were onto her and were fully convinced that she was responsible for Elizabeth being shot.

"We only have a couple more questions for you," the other detective spoke up.

"Go ahead," Elizabeth said, giving them a fake smile. "I want to do everything I can to help."

"We've already established that you believe that Cameron Simms killed your daughter."

"Yes, that's correct." Harmon was very fidgety. She was nervous because she didn't know where this was leading.

"What are your feelings toward Cameron?"

"I hate her," Harmon answered without hesitation. She wasn't going to hide her feelings about Cameron. She was too mad at her to do that. "I think she's a despicable human being. I hope she gets the death penalty for what she did to Allison."

"And you want for us to believe that you have this much ill will towards Cameron but have no negative feelings whatsoever towards her mother? You really want for us to believe that you don't have any problems with Elizabeth when she's been adamantly defending her daughter?"

Harmon just sat there staring at the two detectives and didn't say a word. She didn't know what to say. Her head was spinning from everything that was being said.

"Well, we don't believe it," he continued, closing the notebook he'd been writing notes in. "We don't believe it for a second." With that, the two men got up from the chairs they'd been sitting in and made their way to the door. "We'll be back, Ms. Herrington," he said, the tone of his voice chilling Harmon to the bone. "You mark my words, we'll be back."

Chapter 40

It was almost dark and Peter Herrington was speeding down Laurel Canyon towards the Valley. He was on his way to Joey's Bar, a topless bar he'd learned about from one of the doctors at the hospital. Peter wanted to go somewhere out of the way so that he could be left alone and have a few drinks in peace. He didn't want to run into anyone he knew or be recognized by anyone, so Joey's sounded like just the kind of dive he was looking for. Of course, Peter knew going to a topless bar was a little risky, especially with all the reporters who had been following him lately. It wouldn't look good for him to be photographed in such a seedy place. Peter was willing to take the risk, however. He needed some relaxation time away from everything and everybody he knew. Besides, he was fairly certain nobody was following him right now anyway. He'd been keeping a close watch on his rearview mirror ever since he left Beverly Hills and so far hadn't seen anything suspicious.

Peter was so tired of the media invading his privacy. In his opinion, reporters were nothing but pests and he wished they would all just go away. It amazed him that Harmon didn't agree with him. She loved the paparazzi and their flashing cameras more than anything else in the world. Peter guessed that that came from her being a child actress. She kept telling him that having the media involved to this degree was to their advantage. She said that the bigger deal that Allison's case became to the American public, the more likely the police would be determined to make sure that justice was served.

Peter was now in the Valley and almost to Joey's. He sure hoped this place was everything it was cracked up to be. When he pulled into the gravel lot at Joey's, it was fully dark outside. Peter froze as soon as he got out of his car. Steven's red Mercedes convertible was parked a few spaces down from him.

"Damnit," he said aloud. He had driven all the way out here to get away from everyone he knew and his own son was here. What were the chances of that? Not wanting to have wasted the drive out here, Peter decided to just go ahead and go in. Hopefully, Steven wouldn't notice him and he would be left alone. The parking lot was almost full, so Peter felt the chances of that happening were actually pretty good.

As soon as he entered the dark, musty bar he spotted Steven sitting at the end of the bar making conversation with another guy that was about his age. Peter was lucky. Steven was distracted so he didn't notice him. To cut down on the chances of him even noticing him at all, Peter made his way to the opposite end of the bar by the wall and took a seat. He nodded to the rough-looking man sitting next to him and motioned for the bartender.

"I'd like a Rum and Coke,"

"Sure thing." The bartender hurried off.

Peter quietly surveyed the clientele in the bar. All the men appeared to be a little rough around the edges and most of the women looked cheap. There were definitely no other Beverly Hills plastic surgeons in the place.

"I'm Eddie," the guy sitting next to him suddenly said, extending his hand to Peter. He was wearing a Harley-Davidson jacket and looked like he was ready to jump back on his bike at any moment.

"I'm Peter," Peter said, hesitantly shaking his hand. Eddie was really staring at him as if he was trying to figure something out.

"You look really familiar," he said thoughtfully.

Shit, Peter thought. This guy probably recognized him from all the news coverage. He'd had countless random people he didn't know recognize him in public these past few weeks.

Eddie was still trying to place him when the bartender placed Peter's drink in front of him.

"There you go," the bartender said.

"Thank you, sir."

"I can't remember where I know you from," Eddie said after Joey started talking to another customer. Then it came to him.

"Hey!" he exclaimed. "Aren't you the father of that actress who got killed? That's where I know you from! I've seen you on TV."

"Yeah, I'm Peter Herrington," Peter admitted. "And keep your voice down. I don't want to be recognized by anyone else. People are always bugging me when I go out in public now."

"My bad man," Eddie apologized, genuinely sorry. He knew Peter was going through a hard time and he didn't want to make things worse for him.

"It's okay." Peter didn't look at Eddie but stared straight ahead instead. Eddie got the message that Peter didn't want to chat, so he didn't say anything else to him.

As Peter drank his Rum and Coke, he thought about everything that was going on in his life. He still couldn't believe it all. Two months ago everything was going fine and now he was living in total hell. *Well, things hadn't been exactly peachy two months ago either*, Peter admitted to himself. He *had* been on the verge of suicide, after all. Things were even worse now, however.

Peter was upset about several things in addition to Allison's death. First of all, he was upset about Elizabeth being shot. Even though they didn't have a good marriage and weren't good for each other at all, he still didn't want for her to get attacked like that. She *was* pregnant with his child after all. If she'd been killed the other night, his chance of redeeming himself as a father would have been gone. Having this child was his chance to prove to himself and everyone else that he could be a good father. He'd screwed things up so badly with Steven and Allison, which is why he wanted a second chance. He wanted to do things right this time and actually play an active role in the child's life. He'd never taken the time to spend time with Steven and Allison. That was why he'd never had a close relationship with either of them.

What upset Peter even more than Elizabeth being attacked was the knowledge that Harmon was probably going to wind up being arrested soon. It seemed to him that the police were convinced that she was behind Elizabeth's attack. Peter had to admit that this was the type of thing Harmon would do, but whether or not she actually *was* responsible for it, he didn't know. He had thought a lot about it and had come up with a couple of reasons for why she could have done it, if in fact, she was behind it. One of the reasons she could have done it was because she was so furious that Elizabeth was adamantly defending Cameron. Peter knew that Harmon was still completely certain that Cameron had Allison killed. She told him this almost every time he talked to her lately. Another reason that Peter came up with for why Harmon could have had Elizabeth shot was because she was jealous of her because she was married to him now. Peter could tell that Harmon was still head over heels in love with him and would do anything to get him back. Peter wanted her back too but was a little afraid of her. She really had gotten a lot crazier since they divorced. Peter still couldn't believe that she actually hired a hit man to kill him and had been planning his demise in the weeks leading up to Allison's death. Peter knew that the reason she hired Leonard Holt to kill him was because she didn't want for him to be with another woman if she couldn't have him. It wasn't like she hated him and had some sort of huge vendetta against him like he had originally thought. Peter now knew that Harmon just loved him too much. Her love was like an obsession and Peter was attracted to that. He loved the fact that she lost control when it came to him and did crazy things. It showed him how deep her affection for him was. Peter knew Harmon would do anything to get him back and he found this incredibly hot. She was a dangerous woman and he'd always been attracted to danger. He loved taking risks and living life on the edge. He just hoped she wasn't *too* dangerous.

Peter finished off his Rum and Coke and signaled for Joey to bring him another one. He'd been here for about an hour and the place was starting to get even more crowded. The happy hour crowd was mostly gone and the evening crowd was poring in. Peter noticed that everyone still appeared to be lower-class. He'd yet to spot any Beverly Hills types like himself, except for Steven that is. Peter could see his son still sitting on the other end of the bar. As Peter surveyed the room, he couldn't for the life of him figure out why Steven would like hanging out in a place like this. In his opinion, a guy like Steven shouldn't be wasting his time like this. He wished Steven would start going out to some of the nicer clubs again with his old friends that he'd grown up with in Beverly Hills. The girls were of a much higher quality there than they were out here.

Peter suddenly realized that he was thinking just like Harmon thought. He was being stuck-up just like she always was. He guessed she had rubbed off on him after all those years of being married to her more than he wanted to admit to himself.

The more Peter thought about it, the more he began to believe that Harmon was probably behind Elizabeth's attack. Why else would she have run away to the Hamptons like she did? It didn't make sense that she would leave LA in the middle of Allison's murder investigation. The police had specifically made it a point to request that all parties involved not leave town, but Harmon had done it anyway. Peter realized that behavior like that was sporadic even for Harmon. It couldn't just be a coincidence that she would do something like that immediately after Elizabeth was shot. It made sense that she was involved with the shooting.

Even though Peter didn't agree with Harmon doing something like that to Elizabeth, it didn't stop him from wanting her back. He was more determined than ever to get her back. Peter was glad he'd come to Joey's because he'd made an important decision while drinking and analyzing his problems here. He was going to divorce Elizabeth and get back with Harmon. He knew this was the only way he'd ever be happy again. Although Peter didn't want to stay married to Elizabeth, this in no way meant that he was walking out on being a father to the child she was carrying. He was still going to play an active role in the child's life and be every bit of the father he was supposed to be.

Peter watched as Eddie, who was still perched on the barstool next to him, lit a cigarette. He could see Eddie eyeing him out of the corner of his eye. Afraid that he was about to try to make conversation again, Peter decided to move to one of the nearby tables. A few of them were still unoccupied. As he made his way to the closest table, a hand firmly grabbed his shoulder. Peter whirled around and saw that it was Steven.

"What the hell are you doing here, Dad?" Steven exclaimed, seemingly astounded to see his respectable surgeon father in a topless bar.

"Just having a couple of drinks," Peter replied awkwardly, avoiding making eye contact. He was pissed off at himself for getting up from his place at the bar. Steven most likely would have never noticed him if he'd stayed put.

"Well, let me get us some shots," Steven said, knowing that something wasn't right or his father wouldn't be in a bar like this.

"Sure," Peter said. "Let me pay for it." He shoved a one hundred dollar bill in his son's hand. "Get the strongest thing in the house."

Peter watched as Steven walked up to the bar. In a way, he was kind of proud of himself. He was finally going to spend time with the boy, even if they were just getting drunk together in some shady topless bar in the Valley.

Chapter 41

John was alone in his condo cooking soup for dinner when his cell phone rang. He yelled in dismay when he saw it was his tormentor calling.

"Hello," he yelled into the phone, not at all trying to hide his anger.

"Hi, John," the caller said, sounding extra chipper. "I'm sorry I haven't called the past few days. I've been so busy that I haven't even had time to phone you. I bet you were getting worried that something might have happened to me."

John knew the caller was screwing with him just like he always was. He knew it would be best to try to play it cool like he usually did but he wasn't in the mood for it.

"You know you really are a bastard," he said, surprising even himself. "A cowardly bastard. I mean seriously, man. How long have you been calling me now and you still haven't identified yourself? Come on, this is ridiculous."

"Now, now," said the caller, the tone of his voice unflinching. "Please watch your language, John. There's no need for name calling. You and I are friends. We always have such great conversations."

"We're not friends," John exploded. "Not in any shape or form. You murdered my wife and daughters and ruined my life. I was put on trial for murder because of you."

"I'm not going to stand for being spoken to like this," the caller said, his voice rising. He was starting to lose his temper. He wasn't used to John acting this way. John was usually more passive and easier to deal with.

"You know what then," John yelled furiously stirring the soup. "I'm going to give you exactly what you want. You'll never have to hear me yell and scream again because I'm about to hang up and never take your calls again."

"I wouldn't advise you doing that," the caller said, his voice now strangely calm again. "That would definitely be a bad, bad move on your part."

John wasn't about to back down. He had reached his breaking point with dealing with this monster.

"What are you talking about?" he raged. "What are you going to do about it if I don't answer the phone when you call?"

"I'll come find you sooner than I already plan to, and believe me, you don't want that." He paused and gave a little chuckle. "I'm not exactly the most charming guy in person," he continued. "If your wife and daughters were still alive, they could testify to that."

John couldn't believe what he was hearing. This guy was completely and totally sick.

"That's what I want you to do," he yelled. "That's exactly what I want you to do. I want to come find me. I want you to be a man."

The caller chuckled again.

"If that's really what you want, John, I'll be more than glad to oblige. I might just swing by your little spread in the Hollywood Hills sometime in the next few days. We can have a nice little chat in person. Of course, it might end with the place going up in flames but what I can say, shit happens."

"What do you mean my house might go up in flames? What are you talking about? Is this another one of your threats?"

"Oh no, John," the caller said, his voice colder than John had ever noticed it being before. "It's not a threat…it's definitely not a threat. It's more like a promise, I guess you could say. I'm going to burn your house to the ground."

Chapter 42

Harmon, clad in a swimsuit, was lying in a lounge chair beside the Olympic-size swimming pool behind her house in the Hamptons. She was sipping a margarita Anna had made for her and was trying to act as if everything was okay. In actuality, nothing was okay. Harmon was really and truly scared for the first time in her life. The police were onto her and she didn't know what to do about it. When she hired Leonard Holt to get rid of Elizabeth, she never thought there was even a chance she would get caught.

Elizabeth was in her way more than anyone else had ever been. She was standing in the way of her getting Peter back. Her opinion of Elizabeth couldn't be any lower. She felt that she was nothing but a gold-digging Beverly Hills wannabe. Harmon fully believed that Elizabeth seduced Peter so that she could marry him for his money. She was also of the opinion that Elizabeth had purposefully become pregnant to trap Peter into staying married to her.

Every way that Harmon looked at it, Elizabeth was just in her way. That was why she hired Leonard Holt to get rid of her and her unborn child. She could care less that Elizabeth was pregnant. In fact, the knowledge that she was pregnant made it all the more important that she get rid of her quickly. She didn't want Elizabeth or a child around to prevent her from getting Peter back in her arms where he belonged. Harmon didn't feel the least bit guilty about it. The way she saw it, Elizabeth deserved to die anyway. She had raised a heartless daughter who had had Allison killed for no good reason. On top of that, she was actually defending Cameron and hired one of the best lawyers in the country to try to get her off.

Some good the lawyer is doing her, Harmon laughed to herself. Cameron was still sitting in a jail cell not able to post bail. They must not be too good or she would already be out by now. The thought of Cameron in jail suddenly reminded Harmon of her own predicament. Here she was, in the Hamptons lying out by the pool with the weather gorgeous, and she was probably going to be arrested soon. The police knew she was guilty. They'd sent detectives all the way from LA to question her. It was obvious to Harmon that they were just trying to get enough on her to make an arrest. Knowing that, Harmon wondered if she should run. Life on the run would definitely be better than life behind bars. She had no doubt about that. She would rather die than go to prison.

Harmon really believed in herself enough to think that she could most likely disappear never to be seen or heard from again. Well, there was one person who would hear from her. That person was Peter. She believed that she could convince Peter to meet up with her somewhere later and they could build a new life together with new identities. Everything would be perfect then. It would be like a second chance for both of them. They wouldn't have to deal with any baggage from their old lives that would prevent them from being happy. It would be just the two of them …together forever. The more Harmon thought about it, the more the idea grew on her.

Chapter 43

It was a beautiful day in Los Angeles, but Cameron Simms wasn't enjoying it at all. She had just posted bail and was riding in the passenger seat of her mother's Range Rover. Her mother was driving and Rusty Adams, her lawyer, was in the backseat. They were on their way home where they planned on discussing what was next in this legal mess.

Cameron had never been this depressed in her life. She'd been in jail for three days, and had been completely miserable the whole time. She knew she would do anything to avoid going back to prison. The mere thought that she would have to go back if she got convicted was unbearable. That's why she hoped and prayed that Rusty knew what he was doing, and that this would end well for her.

Cameron still couldn't believe that the police thought she was responsible for Allison's death. She wished more than anything that they could see the truth. She didn't have a bad bone in her body and would never dream of hurting anybody. She would never understand why the authorities reached the conclusion that she was involved in Allison's murder. Allison had been her very best friend since childhood. They'd always been as close as sisters, and actually became stepsisters when her mom married Peter. The friendship Cameron shared with Allison was unlike any of the other friendships she had. She told her everything about herself, and Allison did the same with her. Over the years, they always stuck together through rough times. Allison had been there for her when her dad died and helped her get through it. Likewise, she was there for Allison when her parents got divorced, and didn't abandon her even when she went through her rebellious teenage phase.

They were now creeping through the crowds of reporters and photographers that were standing in front of their house. Her release from prison had been kept extremely quiet, which is why there was only a few reporters who actually witnessed her exit the building. It was obvious to Cameron that those few reporters made some phone calls, because this place was crawling with media.

Elizabeth carefully steered the Range Rover through the crowd and into their driveway. The lights from all the cameras were flashing unmercifully. Cameron couldn't believe what she was seeing. There had to be at least as many reporters here now as there were at Allison's funeral.

"This is absolutely crazy," Elizabeth said, glancing over her shoulder at Rusty as she parked the Range directly in front of the house. "From the way these vultures are acting, you'd think we had the President of the United States in the car."

Rusty nodded his head in agreement.

"The public's interest in this case is huge," he said. "And it's most likely only going to keep growing now that Cameron's been charged."

They all got out of the vehicle, went inside and took a seat at the table in the kitchen. Peter was waiting for them and handed everyone a soda.

"We have a lot to discuss," Rusty said, getting his laptop out of his briefcase. "There are so many different approaches the prosecutor could take to handle this. We're going to have to be ready for anything and everything.

Cameron began to sob. She'd been tearing up ever since they got home, but she'd done a good job of hiding it and maintaining control of her emotions. She couldn't keep up the front, though. Tears were rolling down her cheeks.

"Baby, what's wrong?" Elizabeth gasped, bolting from her chair and rushing to her daughter's side. Rusty and Peter both looked like they didn't quite know what to do. Neither one of them said anything.

Cameron just sat there with her head buried in her hands and didn't answer her mother.

"Cameron, what's wrong?" Elizabeth asked again, her arms lovingly wrapped around Cameron. "Tell me what's wrong."

Cameron uncovered her face and looked directly at her mother. She wasn't hysterical or anything. She was just sobbing lightly.

"I've lost everything," she said. "My best friend, my pride, my reputation, my self-esteem. I don't have anything to live for anymore."

Chapter 44

Steven was getting completely hammered at the beach house. He'd already had half a case of beer and wasn't anywhere close to getting tired of drinking. Consuming this much alcohol was the only way he could dull the pain he felt over all the craziness going on in his life. Steven was drinking in the secret room under the basement so that he could keep Carter company. Carter was completely smashed too.

"So how much longer are you planning on hiding out here?" Steven asked, lighting a cigarette.

"Hell if I know," he said, pausing for a few moments. "Give me one of those cigarettes," he continued, nodding at Steven's pack. Steven handed him one, along with a lighter. He frowned at Carter.

"I can't let you stay here much longer," he said. "You're putting me at risk. If the cops find out I've been hiding you, my ass is toast."

Carter took a drag on his cigarette and inhaled the smoke deep into his lungs.

"You need to chill out, man," he said, taking a swig of his beer. "There's no way the cops are going to find out I'm here. This is the perfect place for me to hide. You're worrying about nothing."

"Carter, you're not thinking logically, man. The cops are probably watching this place closer than we realize. They know we're best friends and that I'm the person that you would likely come to for help." He paused to take a drag on his cigarette. "Secret room or no secret room, it's not smart for you to be here."

Even though Steven was really drunk, he was still thinking logically. Carter, on the other hand, wasn't thinking logically at all. Steven was irritated by this but was trying to control his temper. He'd come to realize over the years that Carter didn't just think illogically when he was drunk. He was pretty much illogical all the time. Steven knew that Carter wasn't too smart and that he thought slowly.

"You're freaking out about nothing," Carter said, popping open another beer. "You need to just calm down."

Steven set his beer down. He could see that he wasn't getting through to Carter, so he was going to have to talk more sternly to him.

"Listen man," he said. "I don't think you get how serious all of this is. The cops want to question you about Allison's murder and you're hiding from them. Do you realize how guilty that makes you look?"

"I don't really care that it makes me look guilty," he said, chugging his beer. "I'm going to move away and change my identity. It's the best thing for me to do at this point."

"That's not true," Steven said, shaking his head. "Running away is not the best way to handle your problems. I've been thinking about it, man. You'd be a lot better off if you just turned yourself into the police and answered their questions. I'm sure that if you did that and they heard from you how much you cared about Allison, they would be able to see that you're innocent."

Carter shook his head in disgust as he lit another cigarette.

"You're wrong," he said. "The cops have already made up their minds. They're convinced that I'm behind Allison's murder and nothing I say is going to make them change their minds. They're on a mission to make sure that I go to prison for this."

"Then how do you explain Cameron's arrest?" Steven asked, completely exasperated. "If the police are really *so* convinced that you killed Allison, then why did they charge Cameron with the crime?"

"I haven't figured that out yet," Carter said. "Maybe it's a ploy. Maybe they're trying to trick me into thinking that I'm safe so that I'll come out of hiding and they can arrest me."

"That's not true man," Steven said. "You're imagining things. That's completely crazy that you think Cameron's arrest might not be real. I really think you've lost it bro."

Steven really did think Carter had lost it. It upset him a whole lot to see what his friend had become. Carter was so paranoid that it almost seemed like he was beyond hope. He was dreaming stuff up and driving himself crazy. Steven watched helplessly as his troubled best friend continued to drink himself into oblivion.

Chapter 45

Peter felt terrible about what he was doing to Elizabeth, but he knew it was for the best. He was sitting aboard a jet on a flight from LA to New York. He was on his way to the Hamptons to be with Harmon… to be with her forever. They were going to change their identities and run off somewhere to start a new life together. It was Harmon's idea but Peter had quickly agreed to it since he'd already made up his mind that he wanted to divorce Elizabeth and get back with Harmon. At first Peter hadn't thought that changing their names and running off somewhere was a good idea because he'd planned on actually being a good father to the baby Elizabeth was expecting. It didn't take him long, however, to realize that escaping their current existence really was what was best for Harmon and him.

Even though Peter felt guilty about abandoning Elizabeth without even saying goodbye, he knew in his heart that this was the only way that his relationship with Harmon had a real chance. In order for their relationship to succeed, they were going to have to start completely over and leave everything behind, including Steven. Peter and Harmon both felt a little guilty about doing this to Steven, but they knew he'd be okay. Even though he'd had a lot of problems over the years, they knew he was a survivor and could make his own way in life without their help. Even though they knew this, they still weren't leaving him financially destitute. Both Peter and Harmon had made plans to have most of their money transferred to a Swiss bank account, but they'd both left Steven with quite a significant sum. He would never hurt for anything. That was one thing Peter knew for sure.

After landing in New York, Peter picked up his baggage and made his way outside of the airport, where Harmon was waiting on him. He spotted her immediately. She was sitting behind the wheel of a black Lexus Convertible that was parked by the curb. The top was down and her music was playing loudly. Peter couldn't help but notice that she looked as hot as ever. She was wearing a bright red designer dress and her eyes were hidden behind Dolce & Gabbana sunglasses. He liked it that she got dressed up to come pick him up. It let him know that she thought he deserved the best.

"Hey there gorgeous," he said as he opened the front passenger door and stepped into the vehicle. He gave her a peck on the cheek. "How are you?"

"I'm doing better," she said, turning the radio off. "Much better. For the first time in a while, I feel like things might actually work out."

She leaned close to him and they began kissing passionately. They both completely lost themselves in the kisses. It had been so long since they'd kissed in such a way. After a couple of minutes of making out, Harmon pulled away from Peter.

"We've got to hurry," she said, putting the Lexus in drive and speeding off in the direction of the East Hampton house. "We've got a lot of stuff to do before we leave town."

"This sure is a nice car you're driving," Peter said, admiring the vehicle in addition to its driver.

"Yeah, you can buy a lot with divorce money," she said slyly. "I bought a Lexus for the Hamptons and a Bentley for LA. I like to ride in style wherever I am." She had a smirk on her face. Peter decided to ignore the comment about divorce money.

"You always did enjoy the expensive things in life," he said.

"I've lived in Hollywood all my life," she said. "What do you expect?"

Peter laughed.

"Yeah, I guess Hollywood will do that to you," he said. "The land of excess and indulgence…La La land"

Harmon was driving at a swift pace so the two of them had wind blowing in their faces. The top to the Convertible was down.

"I'm definitely going to miss LA," Harmon said, brushing her hair out of her face with her hands. "It's essentially all I've ever known. Getting used to living somewhere else is going to be quite an adjustment."

Peter nodded in agreement.

"Same here," he said. "I've lived there for so long now that it's going to be weird to call someplace else home." He paused and had a thoughtful expression on his face. "I'm looking forward to it, though," he continued. "We're about to begin a new Chapter of our lives. We should both be excited."

It wasn't long before they were driving through the front gates of the East Hampton house. They parked directly in front of the house and Anna rushed outside to help Peter with his luggage. He only had a couple of bags since he knew he was leaving everything behind in a couple of days.

As they walked through the front door, Harmon's cell phone rang. She saw it was Steven calling.

"Hello," she answered.

"Hey, have you heard the news?" he asked. He sounded agitated and a little shaken up.

Harmon, who was now walking through the living room towards the kitchen, stopped in her tracks.

"No, what news?" she asked. "What's going on, Steven?"

Peter was staring at her because he could tell that something was wrong. He was frowning with worry.

"Cameron is missing. Elizabeth just called and told me. Apparently, she just disappeared."

Chapter 46

Elizabeth was pacing around her living room completely frantic. John was the only person in the house with her. She hadn't heard from Cameron in over twelve hours. She had called her cell phone repeatedly but there was no answer.

Elizabeth knew that something was wrong. It wasn't like Cameron to disappear like this. There was no way she would run away while out on bail and risk being sent back to prison. She was beginning to wonder if Cameron may have done something to hurt herself. The thought terrified her. She kept trying to push it out of her mind, but it kept gnawing at her no matter how hard she tried to forget it.

Elizabeth still hadn't called the police and reported that Cameron was missing because she didn't want for her to get in huge trouble if she had just run off somewhere for the day. Depending on where she was, it could be a violation of her bail conditions. Cameron had enough to worry about without adding to her problems.

John had told Elizabeth they were going to have to notify the police if Cameron didn't show up within the next few hours, though. She knew he was right. It would be irresponsible for them not to. If Cameron was somewhere thinking about committing suicide maybe the police would be able to locate her before it was too late. Elizabeth and

John were also concerned that maybe whoever killed Allison had either kidnapped or done something to Cameron for some reason. That thought terrified Elizabeth.

"I just wonder where the hell Peter is," Elizabeth exclaimed for what seemed to her like the millionth time. She was worried about Peter too. She hadn't heard from him since this morning, which was weird. Like Cameron, he wasn't answering his cell phone. She'd even called the hospital to try to reach him and they told her that he'd taken the day off.

Elizabeth wasn't nearly as worried about Peter as she was Cameron, though. Peter had been acting very strangely the last couple of days, so him taking the day off work and not telling her about it didn't come as too big of a shock to her. It was obvious to her that he was up to something. She just had to find out what that something was. Elizabeth wondered just where he had snuck off to today.

John had suggested that maybe Peter and Cameron were together somewhere. Elizabeth knew this wasn't the case, though. They weren't that close to each other. There was no way they would have gone off somewhere like this together without telling anybody. That was one thing Elizabeth was sure of. She'd bet her life that the two of them being unaccounted for on the same day was entirely coincidental.

John, who for the past few minutes had been keeping quiet from where he was sitting on the couch, finally spoke.

"I have a feeling that someone kidnapped Cameron," he said. "And I think that someone is the same person who killed Allison. I don't know why I think that. I just do, and I'm usually right when my gut is telling me something this strongly."

"I think you're right," Elizabeth said thoughtfully, her voice tinged with fear. "I just don't think Cameron would have run away like this. Someone had to have taken her. I really think that's what happened."

John listened to what she said. He was greatly impressed with how intelligent Elizabeth acted and how well she conducted herself under such stressful and traumatic circumstances. Even though she was obviously distraught and panicky, she was still able to maintain a certain amount of composure about herself. John was of the opinion that Elizabeth exuded class in every sense of the word.

John's cell phone rang. He looked to see who was calling and shook his head in disgust when he saw who it was. It was his tormenter.

Why does he always call at the worst times? John wondered.

"Hello," he answered, the tone of his voice conveying his annoyance.

"Hi John," the caller said. "I was just calling to let you know that I know where Cameron Simms is. Don't worry about her. She's in good hands. You can tell her mother I said that. She's soon to take her place with Kelly and your daughters." He paused and chuckled. "And we both know that they're in a better place."

Chapter 47

Peter and Harmon were on a private jet headed to the South of France, where they were going to be married. Because Peter was still married to Elizabeth, the remarriage to Harmon wasn't actually going to be made legal. It was going to be more symbolic than anything else. Both Peter and Harmon just wanted to declare their love and dedication to each other in a formal ceremony for the world to see. That was why they were bringing a television crew with them to film the whole thing.

Capitalizing off her newfound fame resulting from Allison's murder, Harmon had made a phone call to a producer friend and told him of her and Peter's plan to run away and have this faux wedding ceremony. She told the producer that they could film the ceremony and didn't have to pay her or Peter a dime for it. It went without saying that the public's reaction to this bizarre turn of events for the Herrington family would be huge. The network that aired it would surely have its ratings shoot through the roof.

The main reason that Harmon and Peter wanted this ceremony to be so public was so that everyone could see how in love with each other the two of them actually were. Over the years, so many people they knew had constantly tried to tell them that they weren't right for each other. These people had said that they should just give up on trying to make their relationship work. For the first time in their lives, Harmon and Peter weren't listening to what other people said. This time they were going to do things *their* way, even if it was unconventional.

What Harmon hadn't told the producer was that she and Peter were going to disappear soon after the ceremony. She felt giddy with excitement every time she thought about how big of a deal it would be with the media when she and Peter went missing. The story would certainly be hashed on CNN, Fox News, and all the other national news networks for months. Harmon believed that she and Peter's disappearance would become legendary, especially if everything went according to plan and they weren't ever found. With all the media attention surrounding Allison's murder, Elizabeth's attack, and Cameron's disappearance in addition to the hype that was going to surround their faux-wedding ceremony, Harmon was confident that she and Peter's disappearance would go down in history as one of the strangest events to ever take place.

The reason Harmon was so excited about all of it was because in addition to getting back together with Peter, she was finally going to become the big star she'd always wanted to be. In a couple of days, she was going to be the most famous woman in the world. She was going to get all the attention she'd ever dreamed of. The fact that she wasn't going to be around to bask in her glory didn't really bother her that much. She would still be able to watch all the news coverage and listen to all the talking heads speculate on what happened to her and Peter. Knowing that her fate would forever be shrouded in mystery to the public was enough satisfaction for her. Harmon could only imagine just how many conspiracy theories the public would come up with. She would be like Marilyn Monroe.

Despite the high level of excitement Harmon felt, she still felt a little guilty about running off before the police found Cameron and locked her back up. She wished that she would be able to go to the trial and watch her get what she deserved, but she knew that if she stuck around for it, that would give the police enough time to gather enough evidence to build a case against her for shooting Elizabeth. Harmon could tell from the way the detectives who had visited her in the Hamptons had talked to her that they were doing everything in their power to make sure that she wound up in prison. She knew it was only a matter of time until she was arrested if she didn't pull a vanishing act.

Peter, who had been sleeping for most of the flight, suddenly stirred and opened his eyes. He looked at his watch.

"We should be getting close," he said, giving Harmon a kiss on the cheek. "I hope France is ready for us."

Chapter 48

John knew something was terribly wrong. It had been over twenty-four hours and they still hadn't seen or heard from either Cameron or Peter. He and Elizabeth were sitting together in Elizabeth's living room talking the situation over and trying to come up with the best course of action.

"I just can't for the life of me imagine where Cameron is," Elizabeth said. Tears were rolling down her cheeks. "I just know something awful has happened to her."

She'd been crying for the last several hours and John had been doing everything he could to console her. He wasn't at his best either, however. Neither he nor Elizabeth had slept since the day before and as a result neither one of them was functioning very well.

"You don't know that for sure," John said, trying to maintain a positive attitude in front of Elizabeth. She needed encouragement and didn't need to know how worried he was about the situation. "For all you know, she could be safe with Peter somewhere."

Elizabeth knew good and well that Peter and Cameron weren't together.

"I know that the two of them aren't together," she said. She had a puzzled look on her face and seemed to John to be confused. He knew the fatigue had to be getting to her.

"This is so unlike Peter to disappear," she whispered, tearing up again. "I bet something horrible has happened to him too."

John didn't respond to her comments about Peter.

"I really think it's time for us to call the police," he said. "At this point I think we're only delaying the inevitable."

"You're right," Elizabeth said with a resigned expression on her face. She was reconciled to the fact that they were going to have to get the authorities involved. She knew it was her best chance of getting Cameron back alive. In her heart, she felt that Cameron had for some reason been kidnapped by Allison's killer. Her gut was telling her that Cameron hadn't hurt herself. She didn't think her daughter would be so selfish as to do something like that and leave her here with so many unanswered questions.

"Do you want for me to call the police or do you want make the call?"

"I'll do it," Elizabeth said, reaching for her cell phone which was on the end table beside the sofa.

Her fingers trembled as she dialed the number and heard it ring on the other end.

"911 Emergency," the operator answered.

"My name is Elizabeth Herrington and I'm calling to report two people missing."

Chapter 49

Cameron Simms had never before been so scared in her entire life. She was locked in a small, windowless room which had been converted into what amounted to a prison cell. The room was completely filthy and smelled horrible. She was able to see out into a narrow hallway through vertical wrought iron bars which covered the entranceway to the room. She could tell that her room was at the end of the hallway but she couldn't see how far the corridor extended in the other direction because the corridor turned not far from her cell. She knew the passageway couldn't go far, though, because she would always hear a door open not too far off in the distance every time one of the men came to see her.

Cameron began trembling all over every time she heard that door open. The men terrified her when they came to visit her. They were all so mean and insulting to her. They yelled degrading things to her and treated her like she was an object. Two of them had already had their way with her, which made her feel dirty and used. Both men had had to use force to rape her because she'd tried so hard to fight them off. Even though Cameron felt powerless and hopeless, it made her feel better to know that she had done everything she could to resist them. Although they succeeded in violating her, at least they had to fight for it. She hadn't just given in to them.

The other men who came to see Cameron didn't ever try to rape her. They only stared at her and told her how stupid and worthless she was. They also frequently told her that they were going to kill her soon, which was causing Cameron to have severe anxiety attacks. They also talked a great deal about Allison, which was why Cameron believed that these people were responsible for her death. Every time one of the men brought Allison up in front of her, they were always careful to not let anything slip that would incriminate them in regards to her murder. They never even mentioned the horrible circumstances of her death. They only talked about how beautiful and nice she'd been. It was obvious to Cameron that these men knew Allison quite well. She couldn't imagine how in the world Allison would have been acquainted with such people, though.

In addition to discussing Allison's great beauty, they also talked about how she had screwed things up for herself and destroyed her future. This is as close as they ever came to talking about what had happened to Allison. Now that Cameron knew these men and knew how they were, she felt even more sorry for Allison than she had before. Something really crazy must have been going on with her for her to be acquainted with people like this. Whatever it was, she hadn't made it out alive.

Cameron wondered if she would make it out alive. It seemed doubtful, considering how they'd been telling her repeatedly that they had plans to kill her soon. What frustrated Cameron the most about the whole thing was that they wouldn't tell her why they had kidnapped her and what exactly it was that they wanted with her. They refused to discuss it even though she had asked them several times. Every time she asked, they started yelling at her to shut the hell up. They also told her that it wasn't her place to ask questions. Not knowing why she had been abducted made it all the more terrifying for Cameron. Without knowing that, she had no way to know who these people were and what their motivations were.

Cameron was still lying on the cot that had been provided for her when she heard the door open and shut down the corridor. She could hear footsteps coming her way. She bounced to her feet and braced herself for whatever was about to happen. When someone came to visit her, it was never pleasant.

Chapter 50

Peter and Harmon had so far enjoyed every minute of their time on Carmichael Reeves' yacht cruising in the South of France. Carmichael, who was one of Peter's best friends from his medical school days, had volunteered his yacht as the place for Peter and Harmon to have their dedication ceremony. Reeves and his twenty-five-year-old wife, Georgiana, had accompanied Peter and Harmon. Reeves was acting as their captain. There was also an elderly couple on board who served as Carmichael's waiter and cook. The couple had worked for him for many years. Several cameramen and Harmon's producer friend were also aboard to film the occasion.

They had been on the yacht for almost a full day now. They'd set sail at 3:00 pm the day before and it was now fast approaching two o'clock in the afternoon. Peter and Harmon were almost ready for the ceremony.

Harmon was below deck with Georgiana, who was helping her get dressed. The ceremony was going to be broadcast live on national television so they had to make certain she looked her best. She wanted to make a good impression on the world, at least as far as her appearance went. Harmon wasn't so stupid to believe that people were still going to have much respect for her and Peter after they went through with this. She was reconciled to the fact that the majority of people were going to think they were horrible people and completely nuts. At least they would know they were in love, though.

Peter was above deck with Carmichael, who was behind the wheel of the yacht. Both men were already in their suits and were waiting for the women to finish beautifying themselves.

"Are you sure you're doing the right thing, Peter?" Carmichael asked. "Don't you think it's kind of low to do something like this on national TV without first at least telling Elizabeth? I mean, think about it. She has absolutely no idea what you're about to do and it's going to affect her life drastically."

Peter gave his friend a go to hell look. He didn't need to hear this right now. The decision to go through with this had already been made and he didn't need someone second guessing him.

"I know I'm doing the right thing," Peter said. "I'm not going to have any regrets. Don't get me wrong. I do feel guilty that Elizabeth is going to be hurt by this. I have to do what's right for me, though. I have to do what's right for Harmon and me."

Carmichael shrugged his shoulders. He had a puzzled look on his face as he listened to his friend try to justify this. It was obvious to Peter that Carmichael didn't agree with what he and Harmon were doing.

Carmichael was a good friend to Peter, however, so he decided not to say anything else about it. He'd already agreed to let Peter and Harmon use the boat for their ceremony, so he knew he shouldn't ruin their big day by trying to shove his personal opinion down their throats.

Peter walked out on the deck where the camera crew was setting up to film.

"Looks like you people are about ready," he said to Arnie, Harmon's producer friend.

"Yeah," Arnie responded, looking at Peter curiously. He wondered what it was about him that Harmon was so attracted to. He'd had a thing for her for years, but she'd never given him the time of day. He didn't understand why, though, because in his opinion he was a lot better looking than Peter Herrington.

When Arnie didn't say anything else, Peter made a second attempt to start a conversation.

"How long have you been in the business?' he asked.

"What business?" he chuckled. "Are you talking about the entertainment business or the business of hiding out on a yacht with a woman who's wanted by the police?"

A chill suddenly ran down Peter's spine.

"What are you talking about?" His voice was shaky with fear. He already had a good idea of what he was about to hear but he didn't want to admit it to himself.

"What I'm talking about," Arnie said. "Is that a warrant has been issued for Harmon's arrest. My wife just called me from the States and told me. She says it's all over the news."

Chapter 51

Elizabeth was sitting on the sofa in her living room crying hysterically. Several detectives and John were present in the room with her. They were all glued to the drama playing out in front of them on TV.

"I just can't believe this," Elizabeth said to John, who was sitting next to her on the sofa to offer his support. "This is absolutely unbelievable."

John didn't say anything but he clasped her hand in his. It hurt him to see Elizabeth in this much anguish. He knew what that meant. He was falling for her. John wanted desperately to be able to protect her and take this pain away from her. He couldn't believe what was happening. It was all a little bit too much too fast.

A few minutes after Elizabeth called the police to report Cameron missing, three detectives had shown up at the house and were asking all kinds of questions about both Cameron and Harmon. Confused as to why they were questioning her about Harmon, Elizabeth demanded to know what was going on. The detectives then broke the news to her and John that a warrant had been issued for Harmon's arrest for shooting Elizabeth. They went on to tell her that when the police went to Harmon's house in East Hampton to make the arrest that the maid informed them that she had gone on a trip overseas with her ex-husband. John would never forget the look on Elizabeth's face when they told her that Peter and Harmon had run off together. She had never before been so shocked and hurt at the same time. It was completely unimaginable for her to believe that Peter would do something like this to her, especially since she was pregnant. She would never understand why he made the decision to do something so horrible. Her head was swimming because she had so many thoughts torturing her.

What did I do wrong, she wondered. *Wasn't I good enough for him? Did I not provide a loving enough home for him. What does Harmon have that I don't?*

While Elizabeth was coming to terms with Peter's betrayal, one of the detectives' cell phone rang. The detective stepped out of the living room to take the call. He was gone for just a few minutes before he re-entered the room with a grave expression on his face. Elizabeth, John, and the other detectives all immediately knew something was wrong.

"What's wrong?" Elizabeth had yelled. Sheer panic could be seen in her eyes. "Is it something about Cameron?"

"No, it's not about your daughter," the detective said. "She still hasn't been located. It's about your husband."

"What's happened to Peter?" Elizabeth exclaimed, expecting to hear the worst. The detective had a sickly look on his face.

"Apparently all the national news networks are reporting that Peter and Harmon are about to have a ceremony to rededicate themselves to each other. Supposedly the ceremony is going to take place on a yacht in the South of France and is going to be aired live on national TV."

Elizabeth had never before in her life been so floored by anything. Ever since the detective told her, she and John had been watching the news waiting for the event to take place. As Elizabeth listened to all the news anchors discussing everything that had happened in her life the past few weeks, she felt completely helpless and hopeless. Everything was spinning wildly out of control and there was nothing she could do about it. Just when she thought it couldn't get any worse it had. As she sat on the sofa next to John, she started to think about things she knew she shouldn't be thinking about right now.

It seemed to her that John was the only person in the world right now who legitimately cared anything about her and Cameron. She hadn't even known him very well prior to a few weeks before which made his caring attitude seem even more remarkable to her. He honestly cared about both the welfare of her and Cameron and didn't seem to want anything in return for his good deeds. Elizabeth had always considered herself to be a good reader of people and she could tell that John was genuinely heartbroken about Cameron's disappearance. She could also tell that it was tearing him up that the police charged her with Allison's murder.

Because John had such a good heart, Elizabeth found herself wondering if anything more than friendship might develop between them. With what was going on right now, it was obvious to her that her relationship with Peter was over. He didn't want anything else to do with her and frankly, she felt the same way at this point. He was a bastard if he would do something like this to the woman carrying his child.

"Here it is," John suddenly exclaimed, reaching for the remote control and turning up the volume on the TV. Elizabeth watched in disbelief as the ceremony began to play out on the screen in front of her.

Chapter 52

Peter's breath was literally taken away by how beautiful Harmon looked when she came on deck just minutes before the ceremony was set to start. She was wearing a gorgeous white wedding dress that she'd had shipped to her from Paris.

"You're so beautiful, Harmon," Peter whispered to her as he clasped his hand in hers. "You look just as beautiful today as you did the day I married you. I can't wait to spend the rest of my life with you."

Harmon was beaming at him. She hadn't felt this happy in years. It was like everything in her life that was wrong, all of the problems she had gone through, was melting away before her eyes. She felt as if everything was finally coming together and changing for the better.

"You don't look so bad yourself, Mr. Herrington," she cooed, giving him a light kiss on the lips. "And I want you to know that I feel the exact same way that you do. I can't wait to spend the rest of my life in your arms. I couldn't imagine spending it with anyone else."

Caught up in the moment, Peter and Harmon both temporarily forgot about the people they were hurting by going through with this. They also pushed out of their minds the knowledge that immediately after they took their vows they were going to have to successfully disappear before the police got the chance to take Harmon into custody.

In the back of their minds, though, they were both well aware that in all likelihood the authorities were already on their way to the yacht to apprehend Harmon. They knew they would have to act quickly if they wanted to get away after the ceremony.

Arnie signaled to Harmon that he was ready to begin the ceremony.

"All of the cameras are in place," he yelled. "All we need now is the happy couple and the pastor."

The pastor was going to be Nelson Hughes, the elderly man who worked on the boat as a waiter. He was an ordained minister and had pastored a Baptist church in Mississippi for years before coming to work for Carmichael Reeves. He'd actually been let go from his duties at the Mississippi church because his beliefs were more liberal than a few prominent members of his congregation. Hughes believed in moral relativism and several other ideologies that Southern Baptists didn't take kindly to. Peter and Harmon both knew that most preachers wouldn't agree to take part in a ceremony such as this one and would deem their actions as sinful. Because Nelson Hughes was non-traditional in his religious beliefs, they knew he was the perfect person to lead the ceremony. They were very thankful that they knew him because it was very important to both of them that their union be recognized by someone who called himself a servant of the Lord.

Hughes, who had been talking with his wife, heard Arnie say that the cameras were ready. He walked over to Peter and Harmon and gave them a big smile.

"Are you two ready?" he inquired.

"I know I am," Harmon said, glancing over at Peter. He gave her a nod that indicated that he was ready to.

"Where do you want us?" Peter asked Arnie, who was busy giving last minute directions to the camera crew.

"I want the preacher guy behind the podium," Arnie said, pointing towards a white podium he had set up on the deck. Decorative flowers were draped across the podium. "I want you standing next to the podium and I want Harmon to be off-camera at first. Once we start filming, I want to show her walking up to the podium with Carmichael Reeves. He's going to be the person to give her away."

They all quickly moved to the places Arnie had instructed them to go. Peter and Harmon had decided to let Arnie basically plan the ceremony in the way that he thought it would generate the most media publicity, which was why they were so eagerly doing everything he requested. In addition to the fact that they both wanted to publicly declare their great love for one another, they also wanted to make sure the event was over the top so that it would go down in history. Harmon had always dreamed of becoming super famous and this could be her last chance to become the legend she'd always aspired to become.

"Okay, everyone's in their places," Arnie acknowledged, yelling so that everyone could hear him. "Lights, camera, action."

Harmon began walking towards Peter, the smile on her face letting him know how deeply she loved him. The ceremony went off without a hitch and was even more beautiful and bizarre than any of them had hoped for. Arnie knew that the story was going to be much bigger than even he had originally thought.

The cameras had now been turned off at the request of Harmon, who wanted the reception to be a private affair. Arnie, Carmichael, Georgiana, Harmon, Peter, Nelson, and the camera crew were all greatly enjoying themselves on the deck of the yacht. They were eating the feast of delicious food that was prepared for them by Nelson Hughes' wife.

As Arnie watched Peter feed Harmon a piece of cake, he shook his head. He knew without a doubt that the two of them were completely and totally crazy. Neither one of them cared about anybody but themselves. He had never met anyone as selfish and heartless as these two. The way Arnie looked at it, they were a perfect match.

Chapter 53

Steven was on his way to Joey's Bar to cut loose and have a few drinks. It seemed like the thing to do since he had a lot on his mind. He was more than just a little upset at the news that his parents went to France and rededicated their lives to each other on national TV without telling him first. He felt betrayed that they'd kept their plan a secret from him and left him out of the ceremony.

Steven was also a little disgusted by the whole thing. Why had his parents felt the need to make such a spectacle of themselves when their family had already been through so much the past few months? Rededicate themselves to each other? What the hell did that mean anyway, especially with the two of them being divorced? The more Steven thought about it, the more ridiculous it seemed. His father was already married to Elizabeth and had now made a commitment to his mom without even first divorcing his wife. It was completely bizarre and didn't make any sense at all. In fact, Steven found the actions of his parents laughable. He had always known they did things their own way, but this was taking it to a whole new level.

Steven felt that it was disrespectful for his parents to have done this to Elizabeth right after Cameron disappeared. It was gross of them and very uncaring. He'd suspected his father wasn't happy in his marriage to Elizabeth, but he'd thought he had more respect for her than to do something like this. Steven felt very sorry for Elizabeth and could only imagine what she was going through right now. The feelings of betrayal and rejection she must be feeling must be horrible. The knowledge that his parents caused this made Steven sick. He was disgusted that they were so selfish. They were always so wrapped up in their own wants and needs. Their selfishness was exactly why they ended up divorced in the first place. His father had wanted a younger and prettier wife and didn't think twice about walking out on Harmon so that he could get what he wanted. Steven knew that his mother was selfish too, which had caused severe problems in the marriage over the years.

Steven felt so bad for Elizabeth that he was actually considering calling her. He knew she really didn't care for him that much so he wasn't sure if he should do it. He wanted to be there for her to offer support if she needed it. She *was* family, after all. *At least for now*, Steven thought. She probably wouldn't be family for much longer. It looked like her marriage to his father had reached the end of its road. As Steven thought about how he would like to be able to help Elizabeth in some way, it dawned on him how much he had matured since Allison died and everything began going wrong for his family. He had learned the importance of family values and realized that there was more to life than getting drunk and high. When his dad first married Elizabeth, Steven had only seen her as an object to lust after. Knowing that she was sleeping with his father hadn't at all deterred him from constantly trying to make a move on her. Now Steven viewed Elizabeth as a human being with feelings and emotions.

Steven also felt this way about Samantha Taylor now. Even though he hardly knew her at all, he wished more than anything in the world that he knew where she was so that he would be able to try to protect her from her problems. The nights he sat drinking in Joey's he'd only admired her because she was physically attractive. He now recognized that she was more than just something to lust after. She was a real woman with real problems and emotions. Steven felt as if she was kind of like a damsel in distress who needed to be rescued by him. He felt a strange need to try harder to find her before it was too late. She'd strangely disappeared after that night she'd talked with him at Starbucks. Steven also couldn't help but believe that if he could talk to Samantha, he would be able to figure out what happened to Cameron. He knew it couldn't just be a coincidence that she vanished so soon after Allison's murder. Steven thought back to the night he had been at Starbucks with Samantha. She had panicked and left before she told him anything substantial. If he wanted to uncover the truth behind Allison's murder, he knew he was going to have to find out what Samantha had almost told him.

Chapter 54

Peter had a buddy named Marlin Wilson back in his college days. Marlin had gone on to become a very successful businessman after their college graduation. He started out with nothing and had built an empire. His business ventures ranged from real estate to casinos. Over the years, Peter had heard rumors that some of Marlin's business deals were less than legal. Some people even said that Marlin had connections to the Mafia. Peter didn't doubt any of it. Back in college, Marlin had been a tough guy who played by his own rules. He'd made his own way in the world playing by these rules.

Marlin and Peter had kept in touch every so often throughout the years and Marlin had often told Peter to contact him if he ever got into any kind of trouble. Peter had known he was in major trouble this time, so he called Marlin and asked him if he could hide him and Harmon somewhere to prevent Harmon from being taken into custody for shooting Elizabeth. Marlin said he knew the perfect place and he sent men to help Harmon and Peter leave Carmichael Reeves's yacht. After that, he had them flown to a private island he owned in the Pacific Ocean. The island was only twenty acres in size and consisted of one large main house and several smaller cabins. Marlin allowed Peter and Harmon to stay in the main house since he knew he wouldn't be using it any in the upcoming months. He sent away the servants who usually resided at the house because he didn't want to risk any of them ratting out the Herrington's to the police.

Peter and Harmon absolutely loved the island. In their opinion, it was the most peaceful place in the entire world…their own slice of heaven. The weather was always sunny and the temperature was hot, which immensely pleased both Peter and Harmon. It was definitely beach weather and the two of them had always loved the beach. When they first got married and things were still very good and loving between them, they would spend hours walking the beaches of Malibu, soaking in the sun. That was before they had kids and began to live separate lives.

Peter and Harmon felt like they had gone back to those days… back when they were young and in love with no real problems to worry about. It was just the two of them on Marlin's island, so they had plenty of time to get reacquainted with each other. They spent most of their time together walking the beaches of the island and just hanging out by the pool behind the main house. They usually made love several times a day. During this time, the only person they ever heard from was Marlin, who called every so often to make sure they hadn't run out of groceries. He'd already flown to the island twice on his jet to bring them groceries and other necessary supplies. Besides Marlin, though, Peter and Harmon had no contact with the real world, and that's the way they wanted it for now. They needed time to get their lives together and figure out what was next for them. Peter and Harmon knew that they would eventually have to leave Marlin's island and start somewhere new with new identities but for now they blocked that realization out of their heads.

Peter and Harmon's long walks on the beach were usually when they had the most intimate conversations. They told each other everything on these walks…most of their dreams and their fears. Both of them wondered why they were never able to talk to each other this openly before. It was almost like it had taken years and years of hurt and pain for both of them to see how much they cared about each other.

Even though they were opening up and being honest with each other, they were both still mentally unstable and unpredictable…

especially Harmon. She was on her best behavior on the island and had confided many of her secrets to Peter, but she wasn't telling him everything. She was hiding her dark side as best she could. She knew that she couldn't let Peter know just how unbelievably mean she could be. She knew that he loved her but she wasn't sure if he would still feel the same way about her if he knew her for who she really was…someone who would kill.

Even though she hired someone to kill Elizabeth, Harmon didn't really think of herself as a criminal. She truly believed that Elizabeth deserved to die. In the back of her head, though, Harmon knew that something must be wrong with her. No normal person could commit the deeds that she'd committed and not feel any form of remorse or guilt whatsoever…even if Elizabeth did deserve to die. It was as if she lacked a conscience. The only time in her life that she'd ever felt guilty about something was when it concerned either Peter or one of her kids. She could care less about anyone else. Sometimes it did bother Harmon that she didn't feel any remorse, but she always quickly pushed these feelings out of her head. She couldn't allow herself to change this late in her life. If she did, she knew she would go crazy with guilt for all the evil she had done over the years.

Chapter 55

Elizabeth was completely bewildered by Peter and Harmon's mysterious disappearance. Under normal circumstances, she would have been devastated by her husband betraying her like this, but these were not normal circumstances. She'd cried and felt sorry for herself a little about it at first but at this point she was numb to the betrayal. She was in survival mode and taking it day by day. She had John at her side full time now. He had moved into the house with her to keep her company and help her out. She'd felt a little weird at first about him moving in with her since she hadn't known him all that long but she quickly got over it. She desperately needed a friend right now and John was the only person around who wanted anything to do with her. All of her other friends and acquaintances had abandoned her in her time of need. Most of them hadn't actually come right out and said it, but Elizabeth got the feeling that the general consensus among these people was that Cameron was guilty of killing Allison and had run off to prevent herself from having to go to prison. They felt like Elizabeth was a bad person because she must have not done a good enough job of raising Cameron.

It made Elizabeth so upset to know that people she had known her entire life thought such horrible and completely false things about her and her daughter. She was a good person and always had been.

Cameron was the same way. She didn't have a mean bone in her body. Elizabeth didn't have any doubt that her daughter had been kidnapped by someone. She believed that that someone was the same person who murdered Allison. To think that Cameron was either being held in captivity or lying dead somewhere when everyone thought she'd run off on her own free will was almost too much for Elizabeth to mentally handle. In her heart, she knew that these people were wrong. Cameron had been taken away by someone and was a victim too. Elizabeth prayed every night that she would be able to prove this someday soon. What she really wanted was for Cameron to turn up safe and sound. Then she herself could tell the world her story and prove everyone wrong. Elizabeth often told John this fantasy when they walked in the garden behind the house every night. Taking a nightly walk through the garden was a part of their routine. The walk was a time when they could escape the confines of the house yet still remain hidden from the prying eyes of the media.

Chapter 56

Elizabeth and John were taking a walk through the garden late one night when Elizabeth excitedly blurted out an idea.

"When Cameron comes home, I want for us to have a huge celebration, John," she said. "The two of us can plan it. We'll invite all her friends."

John looked at his friend with amazement. He could see nothing but hope radiating from her face. Cameron had been gone for a little over four weeks now but Elizabeth was still not faint of heart. She fully believed that her daughter was safe somewhere, alive and well.

John didn't understand where she got her optimism from. It was his belief that the chances of Cameron having a safe return were dismal. She had been gone for too long now and he believed that she had most likely been killed just like her stepsister was. John didn't allow his beliefs to be evident to Elizabeth, though. He didn't want to be discouraging to her in any way.

"Of course we will have a celebration," he said, feeling slightly guilty for playing along with Elizabeth's fantasy. "We'll plan something really nice and everyone will have a great time."

Elizabeth was beaming even more now than she was before.

"Oh John," she exclaimed, suddenly embracing him. "Thanks for believing that it's all going to work out. The entire world thinks that Cameron is dead and they all think I'm completely crazy for holding out this much hope that she's still alive."

It was at that moment that John understood why Elizabeth kept telling herself that Cameron was alive. This hope was the only thing keeping her sane during this difficult time. It was the only thing preventing her from drowning in a sea of depression.

As John and Elizabeth continued to stroll through the garden, she described in detail the celebration she was going to plan for Cameron. It was obvious to John that she had been planning this for quite some time. John listened to her intently and began to realize that he wished more than anything in the world that he could make himself believe the things she was saying. No matter how convincing Elizabeth sounded when she said that Cameron was going to return home safely, he couldn't honestly say that he believed her. He didn't know if that was just because he was being realistic or because he'd seen too much sorrow with his own family's tragedy back in Atlanta. Finding his wife and daughters murdered in their beds and then being falsely accused of the killings had understandably made him a little pessimistic when it came to things like this.

"John, are you even listening to a word I'm saying?" Elizabeth suddenly asked, shaking his arm. "You're just staring off into space with a glazed look on your face." John realized he hadn't been fully listening to her. He'd been too absorbed with his own thoughts.

"I'm sorry," he apologized. "I'm just a little distracted."

"Well, what I'm saying, mister," Elizabeth kidded, "was that I feel like Cameron is going to be coming home to me very soon."

John avoided eye contact with her. He didn't want for her to read his negative thoughts because he didn't want to burst her bubble. He hadn't seen her in this good of a mood since Cameron vanished.

Elizabeth's cell phone rang before she had time to say anything else. She looked at her phone and John could tell from the expression on her face that something wasn't right before she even opened her mouth.

"It's Steven," she said, seemingly bewildered that her stepson would be calling her. "What could he want? I haven't heard from him in weeks."

"Aren't you going to answer it?" John asked. "You better pick up. It could be important."

"Hello," Elizabeth spoke into her phone. Her apprehension was evident by the tone of her voice. John watched as her face went ghostly pale and she began to tremble all over. After talking for less than two minutes, she clicked off the phone.

"Steven's on the way over here," she said. "He says he needs to tell me something important. He says he might have a clue as to what happened to Cameron."

Chapter 57

Elizabeth and John were sitting across the table from Steven in the large kitchen of the Herrington mansion. Steven arrived just five minutes before and they were eager to hear what he had to tell them. Elizabeth was hopeful that he would be able to tell them something significant but John was doubtful. From everything he knew about Steven, he didn't trust him. He wondered if the kid was up to something.

"It's been a while since I've seen you," Elizabeth said, starting the conversation.

"Yeah, I know," Steven said. "I haven't been in LA very much these past few weeks. I've just been hanging out in Malibu trying to stay out of trouble."

Elizabeth noticed a remarkable change in Steven from the last time she'd seen him. He'd lost the cocky attitude and she didn't see any signs of arrogance whatsoever. She wondered what had happened with him to bring about this drastic metamorphosis. John wondered the same thing. The polite young man sitting before him definitely wasn't the Steven Herrington he knew.

"I've been doing a lot of thinking lately," Steven continued, not breaking eye contact with Elizabeth. "I feel like all the pieces to the puzzle are here but I'm having trouble fitting them together. No matter how hard I try, I can't seem to make heads or tails of it."

Elizabeth wasn't following.

"What exactly are you talking about?" she asked, her confusion evident by the puzzled look on her face.

Steven hesitated before he answered her. He wanted to word this carefully because he didn't want to get his stepmother's hopes up. After all, it *was* possible that Samantha was a fraud and didn't really possess any significant information about Allison that could lead them to figuring out who was behind her murder and Cameron's disappearance.

"I feel that there's a good chance that we have enough information to figure out who killed Allison and kidnapped Cameron," he continued. "There's a girl named Samantha that I kind of know and I think she may know something about all this." Steven watched as Elizabeth hung on to his every word. He also couldn't help but notice that John was thoroughly taking him in.

"Who is this Samantha?" Elizabeth asked. "How do you know her?"

"I met her at a bar called Joey's Bar in the Valley. This was a couple of weeks before Allison was killed. She was with two of her girlfriends and she just randomly came up to me and started making conversation."

Steven was talking very slowly as he tried to remember exactly how his first encounter with Samantha went. Elizabeth was getting a little frustrated with him because it seemed to her that he was taking his sweet time relaying the story and she felt like she was pulling it out of him.

John was still sitting back not saying a word. He was taking everything in and making sure he understood what Steven was saying. He could tell by the way that Steven was acting that this conversation was legitimate and that he wasn't just up to no good. John was no longer a skeptic. He didn't know what it was that Steven was about to tell them but he knew it was something big.

Steven continued on with his story.

"I saw her a few more times after Allison died…every time she came up to me and acted extremely weird and purposefully mysterious. When I would talk with her, I would get the feeling that she was trying to tell me something about Allison."

Elizabeth was more frustrated and confused than ever.

"I'm sorry, but I'm still not following you, Steven," she said exasperatedly. "Why did you think she was trying to tell you something about Allison? Just because a girl comes up to you in a bar and acts a little weird doesn't mean that she has information about your sister's murder."

It was then that Steven realized he'd left out the most important part of the story.

"I'm sorry," he said, shaking his head at his own stupidity. "I'm a little rattled with trying to remember all this. Anyway, one night when I saw her at Joey's I asked her to come with me to a Starbucks a couple of blocks away. She came with me and while we were there she told me that she needed help and that she thought that I was the only person who could help her. Samantha was crying and said that she was afraid she was going to get herself in too deep and wind up like Allison."

Hearing this literally gave Elizabeth chills. It seemed to her that Steven was on to something. She felt so hopeful hearing this because she'd almost begun to lose hope. She hadn't conveyed that to John or anyone else for that matter, though.

"What else did she say?" Elizabeth asked excitedly.

"That's all she said," Steven answered. "She panicked after she said it and refused to elaborate on what she meant. It wasn't long after that when she went running out of the Starbucks. I've tried to find her since then but haven't had any luck."

Elizabeth felt a churn in the pit of her stomach.

"What do you mean, you've tried to find her?" she asked, crestfallen. "Where is she?"

"I have no idea," Steven said. "That's the problem. For a while there I started hanging out at Joey's all the time hoping that I would run into her. I never did, though, so I finally gave up on it. No one I ask about her seems to know who she is."

"We have to find her," Elizabeth exclaimed, looking desperately at John. "If she can tell us who killed Allison, we will find out what happened to Cameron. I know in my heart that Cameron's disappearance is related to Allison's murder."

"Someone's got to know who Samantha is and where she is right now," John said thoughtfully.

"Someone does know who she is but I don't think he's going to tell us what we need to know."

"Who?" Elizabeth asked.

"Joey…the guy who owns the bar. She says that she's his niece. For whatever the reason, though, he denies knowing her."

Elizabeth and John looked at each other in disbelief. This was getting weirder and weirder by the minute.

John stood up and looked at his watch.

"It's ten o'clock," he said. "We need to go out to Joey's right now and talk to this guy. He's our best hope of finding Samantha so that she can help us."

Elizabeth and Steven followed John out to his car and they all got inside. They both knew John was right. Getting Joey to open up to them was their only hope.

Chapter 58

When John, Elizabeth, and Steven pulled into the gravel parking lot of Joey's Bar, a very different scene than they expected awaited them. About a dozen police cars with their lights flashing were sitting in front of the building. Uniformed officers and other authorities were busily moving around everywhere, many coming in and out of the bar, which had been taped off with yellow crime scene tape.

"What the hell is going on here?" Steven said.

One of the officers knocked on John's BMW window. John rolled down the window.

"The place is closed," the officer said. "You people need to go ahead and get on out of here. There's been a murder."

"A murder," Elizabeth gasped. For some reason she was surprised, although from the number of officers present, she knew she shouldn't be. It was obvious when they pulled up that something really bad had happened.

"Who was murdered?" John asked. The officer, who had already begun to walk away from the car, turned around and shot John a look that let him know he was annoying him.

"The guy who owns this place. Now go on and get out of here."

John nodded and backed his car out of the parking lot. He drove back in the direction of Beverly Hills. For a while, none of them said a word, however, all three of them were thinking the same thing.

Steven was the one who finally broke the silence.

"This isn't just a coincidence that Joey was murdered, is it?" he asked.

"It could be," John said, trying his best not to jump to the conclusion that he already knew in his heart was the truth.

"No, it's not a coincidence," Elizabeth spoke up, not wanting to waste her time trying to convince herself that it was. She knew that there was no way that Joey's death could be a coincidence.

"This is definitely not a coincidence," she said again. "Think about the facts here. First, Allison was murdered and then Cameron disappeared. It seems to me that Allison's killer was afraid that Cameron knew something that could lead to the killer's identity, so Cameron had to be dealt with too."

Elizabeth paused for a few seconds. She realized that she had just virtually said aloud that Cameron had probably been killed. She knew that it was good for her to admit this to both herself and to others because it was most likely the case and she needed to come to terms with it. Also, Elizabeth knew that the sooner she stopped living in a fantasy world of false hope, the more likely it was that she would be thinking more clearly and be able to recall something that could help the authorities solve these cases. She felt like Steven said he felt, like the pieces of the puzzle were right in front of her, but she just wasn't fitting them together correctly. Elizabeth continued talking.

"Then this Samantha girl who suddenly appears and implies that she knows something about Allison's death seemingly runs away and her uncle is murdered not long after that."

"Yeah, I think you're right, Elizabeth," John said, bringing the car to a halt at a red light. "There's no way that all of this is a coincidence. I think we should go back to Joey's Bar and tell the police there what we know."

"No, I don't want to do that," Elizabeth said with a look of determination on her face. "The police have done nothing to help me. They are convinced that Cameron killed Allison and skipped town to avoid going to prison. I want for us to figure out what's going on our own without involving them."

John was a little more skeptical, but decided not to voice his opinion. After all, he hadn't been able to trust the police very much himself ever since he was falsely accused of murdering his wife and daughters.

"If you don't want to go to the police, then we won't go to them," John said as he turned onto Mulholland Drive.

"Do you agree?" he asked Steven. He made eye contact with the boy through the rearview mirror.

"Yeah, I'll do whatever you two want to do. I think we can solve this on our own without assistance from the police."

Elizabeth nodded her head in agreement.

"You're exactly right," she said. "And our first step is going to be tracking down this Samantha girl."

The conversation was interrupted by the ringing of John's cell phone. When he saw it was the stalker calling him, he cursed aloud but decided to answer anyway.

"What the hell do you want?" he answered through gritted teeth. He was clutching the steering wheel so tightly that his knuckles had turned completely white.

"Well hello there," the familiar voice said. The tone was taunting as usual. "How was your trip to the Valley? Things were a little wild at Joey's tonight, weren't they?"

Chapter 59

Peter and Harmon were walking on the beach late one night deep in conversation and more in love than ever. They were telling each other little things about each other that they had never told before. Peter told Harmon about the time when he was ten-years-old and ran away from home for a couple of days only to be caught by the police and sent right back to his parents. Harmon told Peter about the time in middle school that she sent herself flowers on Valentine's Day with a card signed "your secret admirer." She'd had the flowers delivered to her while she was at school so that her classmates would think an older boy was chasing her. Peter and Harmon's moods were both light as they shared these stories. The reason they were so jovial was because they knew that time spent like this was allowing them to truly get to know each other all over again.

As they talked, Harmon began to wonder what Peter's reaction would be if she told him something a little more dark about herself. She couldn't help but wonder if he would be scared off because she felt like most men would probably be. She hoped that he wouldn't be scared off, though, because she believed that if he truly loved her, he would accept her completely just as she was. Because she felt that it was important for her to know just how much he cared for her, Harmon decided to confess something to him that she had never confessed to anyone before. The way she looked at it, this was a test.

She decided to broach the subject carefully at first so that she could feel him out a little and maybe get an idea of what his reaction might be before she laid all of her cards down on the table.

Chapter 60

Steven decided to temporarily move into the Beverly Hills house with Elizabeth. He thought it was best if they stuck together until the murders stopped. Elizabeth felt the same way. They were both aware that it was a very real possibility that one of them was going to be next. In addition to fearing for his life, Steven was also having trouble coming to terms with the knowledge that both of his parents had completely abandoned him. He'd known for a while that they weren't exactly the closest or most normal family but he never imagined that his parents were capable of just walking out of his life without so much as a goodbye. The fact that they deposited over four million dollars in his checking account right before they disappeared did little to alleviate his feelings of betrayal. Steven also felt really sorry for Elizabeth and resented his parents for doing this to her. The poor woman was about to have a baby and didn't deserve to be abandoned. It made matters even worse that Cameron disappeared at the same time.

Steven saw that John was basically the only good thing in Elizabeth's life right now. Steven couldn't help but like John when he saw how much he was helping Elizabeth. When John was living with his mother, he'd hated his guts. He hadn't given him a chance and had treated him very unfairly. Steven now saw how stupid he'd acted and had apologized to John for acting like such a jerk to him.

It was late in the afternoon a couple of days after Joey was killed when Steven, Elizabeth, and John were sitting at Elizabeth's kitchen table discussing things.

"We've already established that Joey's murder couldn't be a coincidence," John said. "Whoever killed Allison and kidnapped Cameron must have killed Joey because he was afraid that Joey knew about whatever Samantha was involved with. We know from Samantha herself that she was involved with something that she was afraid would get her killed. She said that 'she didn't want to wind up a victim like Allison.'"

"I wonder if it has something to do with drugs," Steven said. "What else could get them killed?" Steven silently doubted Carter for the first time. Maybe he *was* somehow involved in this. He was definitely all into drugs and associated with a lot of drug dealers in the Los Angeles area.

"I have a hard time believing that Allison would have done drugs," Elizabeth chimed in. "I mean I know she wasn't the perfect child but as far as I know she never had any kind of problem with drugs."

"But she dated someone who does do drugs," John said thoughtfully. "When Allison began dating Carter, she may have unknowingly stepped into a world of drugs that she didn't even know existed. Someone could have murdered her to get even with Carter over a drug deal gone wrong. The possibilities are endless. Who knows what could have happened?"

"He's right," Steven said, beginning to feel guilty for harboring Carter. "There's no telling what kind of trouble Carter could have gotten her into."

"Whoever killed Allison may have also kidnapped Cameron as a way to get back at Carter since she was carrying his child," John said.

Elizabeth noticed John's use of the word 'was' but didn't say anything. Now it seemed that he too had given up hope that Cameron was alive. Steven decided to speak up and voice some concerns he was having.

"I don't want for us to make the mistake of completely focusing on Carter," he said. "It's still possible that he might not have one thing to do with this. If we focus on him and his drug dealing friends and they really don't have anything to do with it, then the real culprit will get away. That's the last thing we want to happen."

John nodded his head in agreement.

"You're right. If we're going to keep trying to figure all this out, then we're going to have to keep an open mind and be open to any and all possibilities."

"I agree," Elizabeth said. "I don't want to just find someone to blame for this like the police and the media seem to want to do. I want to know the truth."

"Now that Joey is dead, he can't lead us to Samantha," John said. "So what's our next step?"

"Carter," Steven said. "He's our next step. We have to talk to him."

"But he's disappeared," Elizabeth said, staring at Steven like he was a moron. "We can't talk to him because we don't know where he is."

Steven didn't say anything for a few moments but then decided to come clean.

"I know where he is," he said, getting up from his chair at the kitchen table. "Come on, let's go. We're going to Malibu."

Chapter 61

With Steven driving, they made the trip from LA to Malibu in record time. It was nearly midnight, so there weren't many other drivers on the Pacific Coast Highway. When they pulled up to the beach house, it was pitch black. Elizabeth looked at Steven doubtfully.

"It doesn't look like anyone's home," she said.

"He's here," Steven responded, bringing the Mercedes convertible to a stop at the front door. "He's in the secret room under the basement."

"There's a secret room under the basement?" Elizabeth exclaimed. "How do I not know that and this is my beach house?"

Steven shrugged his shoulders.

"I don't know," he said. "It must have slipped Dad's mind to tell you about it. The people who used to live here told us about it when we bought the place." Steven paused. "That was before you and Dad got married, though. He was still married to my mom then."

Steven, Elizabeth, and John got out of the car and walked into the house. Steven flipped on lights as they made their way through the house and down the staircase to the basement.

John was taking in his surroundings. The opulence of the place amazed him. This house was almost as nice as the house in Beverly Hills. The Herrington's lived like no other people he'd ever met.

John and Elizabeth followed Steven into a small workshop. The walls were lined with shelves of tools, some of which appeared to be very old. Steven walked over to the back wall and pulled on one of the shelves. The wall opened up like a door to reveal a spiral staircase which led below the house.

Elizabeth gasped.

"I can't believe I didn't know about this," she said. "I've been in this room numerous times before and never suspected anything."

John and Elizabeth were now following Steven down the steep staircase.

"Who's there?" a voice called out. Elizabeth instantly recognized the voice as belonging to Carter.

"It's me," Steven yelled. "I've brought my stepmother and John Parker with me."

"Why the hell do you have them with you?"

Steven could hear the panic in Carter's voice. He thought he'd been ratted out and was probably about to be arrested.

"How could you do this to me, man?" Carter yelled out before Steven could say anything. "I thought we were like brothers."

Elizabeth and John exchanged worried expressions. They hoped this wasn't about to turn into a confrontation.

"Don't worry, man," Steven said, opening the door which led to the windowless room where Carter was. "I haven't rat you out to the police. You know I wouldn't ever do that without good reason."

John and Elizabeth were standing behind Steven silently examining the small room they were in. Carter was sitting on a cot and appeared to be both a little drunk and a little high. Beer cans littered the floor and John was almost certain that the white powdery substance on the small table beside the cot was cocaine.

Carter was no longer panicking but he appeared to be very angry with Steven. He was glaring at his friend and he kept shooting not so discreet glances at John and Elizabeth.

"What are they doing here?" he demanded. "I thought we agreed not to tell anyone where I'm hiding."

"We did agree to that," Steven said. "But that was before I got to thinking."

"Thinking about what?"

"That maybe you might know something about Allison's death or Cameron's disappearance that you haven't told me."

Carter jumped off the cot and punched the table in anger.

"I don't know shit," he exploded. "I can't believe you're walking in here with these people acting like I killed your sister. You're my best friend, man. You of all people know how much I loved Allison. She meant everything to me." His anger had quickly dissipated and now tears were running down his cheeks. He was sobbing so hard that Steven, John, and Elizabeth could hardly understand what he was saying.

"She's the only girl that ever gave a shit about me," he continued. "How could you possibly think that I would hurt her?"

Steven was shaking his head at Carter.

"You've got it all wrong," he said. "I don't think you killed Allison. I'm just wondering if maybe some drug dealer is trying to get back at you by doing bad things to the people that you're close to. You have to admit that it's kind of weird that when two girls were pregnant by you, one of them got murdered and the other one disappeared."

"Why would a drug dealer be trying to get back at me? Get back at me for what?"

"I don't know. You tell me."

"I haven't done anything to piss off any drug dealers. As far as I know, none of them have anything against me."

"As far as you know," John said, speaking for the first time since he'd entered the room. "But I guess there could be things that you don't know, especially since we're talking about drug dealers here."

Carter scowled at John.

"What the hell do you know about any of this?" he asked.

John didn't say anything. He only stared at the boy and wondered how he'd gotten so screwed up. Despite Carter's bad attitude, John couldn't help but feel sorry for him. When John didn't respond, Carter again turned his attention on Steven.

"You never answered my question, Steven," he said.

"What question?"

"I want to know right fucking now why you brought John and Elizabeth here."

"I brought them because together we're trying to figure out who is behind these crimes. Elizabeth, as you already know, is Cameron's mother and would like some answers as to what happened to her daughter.

"Well, you're not going to find your answers here," Carter said, wiping the tears from his eyes. "You're looking in the wrong direction."

Elizabeth decided to speak.

"Do you know a girl named Samantha?" she asked Carter. "She hangs out sometimes at Joey's Bar in the Valley."

"She's Joey's niece," Steven chimed in, closely watching his friend to see if he seemed to recognize the name. Carter showed no sign that he did.

"I don't know who you're talking about," he said. "I didn't even know that Joey Bennett had a niece. Why are you asking me about her anyway? What's she got to do with any of this?"

Steven decided to explain.

"I've talked to her several times at Joey's Bar and one time we left Joey's together and went to Starbucks. She alluded to the fact that she may know something about Allison's death. I want to talk with her again so that I can try to find out what she was talking about."

"Talk to her again, then," Carter said. "Maybe she'll tell you some-thing that will lead you in the right direction and get you off my ass."

"I would talk to her if I knew where she was," Steven said. "That's the problem, though. I haven't been able to find her."

"Ask Joey where she is. You said she's his niece."

"Joey's dead," John broke in. "He was murdered the other night."

Chapter 62

"What the hell?" Carter exclaimed, falling back down on the cot in shock. "Joey's dead?" He seemed to not be able to believe what he was hearing.

"Yeah, someone killed him inside his own bar," Steven said, his face bleak. "The police think someone was waiting on him when he came back into work to get the bar ready for the night. One of the back windows was busted out, so they think that's how the person entered the building."

Steven had learned all this from the newspapers which he'd read the next day to get all the details.

"The police didn't catch the person who did it?"

"Not yet," Elizabeth said, once again contributing to the conversation. "Hopefully they will, though. A crime that violent should not go unpunished."

Carter shook his head in disbelief.

"I can't believe someone did something like that to Joey. He was such a great guy. He was always so friendly and fun to be around."

"Someone didn't think so," John said solemnly. "We think someone thought he knew too much."

Carter looked a little confused.

"So you're saying that you think there's a connection between Allison's death, Cameron's disappearance, and Joey being killed?"

Steven nodded his head.

"That's exactly what we're saying," he said. "Think about it, Carter. It can't just be a coincidence. Let's go over the details. First, Allison was murdered. Cameron was then accused of murdering her and subsequently disappeared. In the meantime, this girl named Samantha claims to know what happened to Allison. Not long after that, Samantha drops off the face of the earth and her uncle is murdered shortly after that."

"I think you're right," Carter said with a thoughtful expression on his face. "The same person is behind all of these crimes."

"Or group of people," Elizabeth said. "I'm beginning to think that multiple people are involved. This is too much for one person to be doing by themselves."

John had been sizing Carter up ever since he'd entered the secret room. After talking with him, he definitely didn't believe that he was behind Allison's murder or Cameron's disappearance. The poor kid was too strung out on drugs to pull off crimes that big. John also didn't believe that Carter had any knowledge of who might be responsible for the murder or disappearance. He felt confident that the boy wasn't concealing any information about drug dealers who may have vendettas against him. John could tell that Carter honestly believed that no dealer was out to get him.

Whether or not a dealer really was out to get him, however, John had no way of knowing. Although Carter was confident that one wasn't, John was not so confident. He felt that it was very possible that some drug dealer with a grudge against Carter had killed Allison and then kidnapped and probably killed Cameron. Both girls were pregnant by Carter, so the dealer would have been assuming that he was really hurting the kid. It probably made it even better for the person behind everything that Carter had to go into hiding because the police believed him to be the killer. The culprit probably really thought he'd ruined Carter's life now.

As John listened to Steven and Elizabeth continue to carry on conversation with Carter, John stared at the guy in pity. He couldn't help but feel sorry for him. It seemed that he was being falsely accused by both the police and the media. Considering John's past, he had no tolerance for this type of thing. He knew firsthand what it was like to be wrongly suspected of committing a crime and he didn't want for anyone to have to walk in his shoes. John could now see that Carter and Cameron were in the exact same situation. They were both being harassed for something they didn't do. John promised himself that he was going to do his very best to try to figure out who was responsible for the crimes, not only for Cameron but for Carter too.

Suddenly realizing how completely exhausted he was, John looked at his watch. It was a little past two in the morning.

"Don't we need to get back to LA?" he asked. He was talking to Steven and Elizabeth. "It's really late and I'd like to get some sleep."

Steven glanced at his watch and when he saw the time it dawned on him that he was really tired too.

Elizabeth shook her head at John.

"I think it's best if we just crash here tonight," she said. "If some reporters happened to have followed us here, they'll get suspicious that something is going on if they see us driving back to LA this late. They'll wonder why we drove out here in the first place and might start sneaking around the house or something."

Steven agreed.

"She's right," he said. "The last thing we need right now is for someone to start sneaking around out here and discover that we've got Carter stashed away. We'd be arrested as accomplices."

"Ok, we'll just stay here tonight, then," John said. "We can head back to LA in the morning."

Chapter 63

Steven decided to take Mulholland Drive back to LA instead of the Pacific Coast Highway, which is the way they had come.

"I haven't been this way in a long time," Elizabeth said with a yawn.

"I haven't either," John said. "I always take the PCH." He was yawning too and looked extremely tired. None of them had slept very well at the beach house after talking with Carter. They had so many thoughts running through their heads.

One of Elizabeth's main concerns at this point was being arrested as an accomplice for hiding Carter in her beach house. She'd already mentioned it to John and Steven a couple of times since they'd left Malibu.

"I just don't have a good feeling about it," she said once again. "All three of us are going to jail if the police ever find out that we knew where Carter was but we didn't turn him in."

"I really think you're worrying too much," Steven said. "There's no way the police are ever going to know we knew where he was. The police aren't even going to get a chance to talk to him. He's going to run away and start a new life under a new name as soon as all of this dies down."

Elizabeth looked at Steven like he was stupid.

"And what if the police eventually catch him and he tells them that you hid him in our house and that John and I knew about it?" she asked. "What if that happens?"

Steven shook his head.

"That would never happen," he said. "I've known Carter all my life and I know that he would never betray me like that. I have full confidence that he would never tell the police that he hid in our house or bring us into it in any way. He wouldn't allow us to go down for helping him out."

Elizabeth looked doubtful and so did John.

"I don't know if I have as much confidence in Carter as you do, Steven," John said. "That's beside the point, though, because if we did turn him in to the police, we wouldn't be doing the right thing." John paused and stared out the window thoughtfully. "After talking to him, I have no doubt that he's innocent. If we turn him in to the police, there's no telling what would happen to the guy, especially now that Cameron has disappeared and can't be their scapegoat. They're liable to drum up charges and put him on trial for crimes he really didn't commit. I'm not going to let what happened to me happen to Carter."

Steven took his eyes off the road and looked over at John in confusion.

"What do you mean, you're not going to let what happened to you happen to Carter?" he asked. "What are you talking about?"

Elizabeth was curious too.

"Yeah, what are you talking about?" she echoed Steven from the backseat.

"I don't know," John stammered, obviously flustered. "I'm just rambling at this point. I need to just calm down."

Steven made eye contact with Elizabeth through the rearview mirror. Neither of them was convinced that John was telling the truth but they decided not to press the point.

They were driving through the streets of Beverly Hills now and were almost home.

"What's our next step?" Elizabeth asked John. "What are we going to do when we get back to my house?"

"I think the first thing we need to do is get some proper sleep," John said. "We didn't sleep well last night and we're not going to solve anything until we get a few solid hours of sleep."

"I agree with John," Steven said. "We need to crash for a few hours then come up with a game plan."

"I guess you're right," Elizabeth said reluctantly. "We can sleep until mid-afternoon and then get up and try to be productive."

They were driving through the gates to the Herrington mansion when John's cell phone rang. The words 'private call' flashed across the screen.

"Shit," he said aloud, staring at the phone. It was the caller…just about the last person he wanted to talk to right now.

"What?" Elizabeth asked, leaning forward towards John. "What wrong?"

John ignored her as the phone continued to ring. He was deep in thought. He'd been pondering an idea he'd come up with several days ago and decided to go ahead and act on it.

What the hell? John thought as he answered the phone. *It just might be crazy enough to work.*

Chapter 64

"Why hello there, John," the caller said, his voice sounding extra chipper today. "How are you?"

"I'm fine," John answered through gritted teeth. "I was wondering when you were going to call again. It's been a couple days since we've talked." He was trying his best to be a little nicer than usual with the hopes that the idea he'd come up with would work.

"Oh, you shouldn't have worried, John," the caller said with a slight laugh. "You should have known that I would call again soon. There's no way I'm going to forget about you."

The caller paused for a moment and then continued.

"Now, tell me how Elizabeth and Steven are doing. Did the three of you have fun on your little jaunt out to Malibu?"

John glanced down the driveway towards the street to see if he could see anyone watching them. There was no one in sight. He noticed that both Elizabeth and Steven were both staring at him oddly as they listened to the conversation.

"Say something, John," the caller said, the tone of his voice taunting. "Why so silent all of a sudden?" Surely you're not actually surprised that I followed you?"

"No, I'm not surprised at all that you followed us," John responded. "I am a little surprised that one of us didn't spot you, though."

John looked at Elizabeth through his rearview mirror and could tell by her panicky facial expressions that she was freaking out that someone had followed them. He knew how worried she was that someone was going to find out that they knew where Carter was.

"I have no idea why you're surprised that you didn't spot me," the caller said with a laugh. "If you haven't spotted me all these weeks, I seriously doubt you're going to start now. Let's just say that I'm very skilled at remaining incognito."

"You obviously are," John said, beyond irritated but desperately trying not to lose his temper. He decided to go ahead and pitch his idea to the caller. There was no use in wasting time with idle chatter.

"I think it's time that the two of us get together and meet," John said. "You've been calling me all this time. I think we need to get better acquainted."

John realized now that the caller was too smart for him. It looked like the only way he was going to find out his identity was to arrange a meeting with him. Playing detective wasn't getting anywhere.

"Don't bullshit me, John," the caller said with a laugh. "I'm not stupid. You're not interested in becoming better acquainted with me. You're only interested in finding out who I am so that you can turn me in to the police."

Now it was John's turn to laugh.

"Hold on just a minute," he said into the phone. He looked over at Steven and then turned around to face Elizabeth. "Can you and Steven go ahead and go inside?" he asked. "I've got some private business I need to discuss." Elizabeth, whose eyes were wide, nodded her head and got out of the vehicle. Steven quickly followed suit but was staring at John suspiciously. He wondered what was going on and thought that he may have trusted this guy too soon.

John rolled down his window.

"I'll explain everything to both of you in a little while," he yelled after them as Elizabeth unlocked the door to the house and she and Steven went inside. Once the door had closed behind them, John resumed his conversation. He could hear the caller chuckling about him asking Elizabeth and Steven to leave.

"Part of what you said is true," John said. "But part of it is false. You're right about me not wanting to get acquainted with you. I really don't have any desire whatsoever to get to know you. It's not like we stand a chance of becoming friends or something, which is understandable considering you killed my wife and daughters. You're also right about me wanting to find out who you are. What you're wrong about, though, is thinking that I'm going to turn you into the police."

The caller wasn't buying it.

"Oh yeah," he exclaimed. "And just why should I believe you? Give me one good reason to believe that you're not going to turn me in to the authorities."

Chapter 65

Elizabeth felt like her whole world had crumbled around her. The only person who was really there for her was John. She felt a little weird at first leaning on him to help her get through all of her problems. The reason for that was because she hadn't known him very long. At this point, though, their friendship had developed so much that she felt like she'd known him for years. He'd been by her side ever since Cameron disappeared and she trusted him implicitly.

There had still been no news from Cameron, so Elizabeth was beginning to fear the worst. She still hadn't really voiced her fears to John yet, however, because she didn't want to admit just how defeated she felt. She was so worried about Cameron that she could hardly eat or sleep. When she did manage to eat, a lot of the time she couldn't keep it down and when she slept, she endured the most terrifying nightmares she'd ever had. She dreamed of all kinds of horrible things that could have happened to her daughter. Elizabeth was fairly certain she was experiencing anxiety attacks too because several times lately she had hyperventilated about Cameron to the point of hardly being able to breathe. She didn't think that John had noticed this, which she was thankful for. She didn't want for him to think that she was weak. All of her life, Elizabeth had put her best face forth to the world and she refused to do differently now. She wanted to be perceived by the police, the community, and the media to be a strong woman fully capable of getting through this crisis. She was born a fighter, so this attitude came natural to her.

Ever since Peter and Harmon ran off together, the media coverage of the case had more than tripled. Members of the Herrington family were now household names across the globe. The world was completely fascinated by the mysterious disappearance of Cameron just after she posted bail after being charged with Allison's murder. Elizabeth knew the reason there was so much interest was because Allison's movie, *Deceptive Intentions*, was now in theaters across the United States. Because of Allison's murder and the resulting events concerning the Herrington family, the movie was a box office smash, having come in at number one each week for the past month and grossing over one hundred million dollars so far. There was even talk that Allison might win an Oscar posthumously for her work on the film.

Elizabeth also knew that another reason there was so much interest in the case was because of Harmon's past as a child television star. There were so many people who could remember her as the cute little girl who was in so many television shows. These people couldn't believe that the little girl they had all loved so dearly was now living a life marred with such sorrow and tragedy. Most of the media was saying that Harmon must be unstable to have run away with her ex-husband. Elizabeth agreed with these people. She believed that Harmon was a very unstable woman. She also believed that she was desperate, which made her dangerous. Elizabeth knew that Harmon was desperate to get Peter back and to make certain that Cameron was convicted of killing Allison. It scared her to know that Harmon had already accomplished one of those goals and had been well on the way to accomplishing the second when Cameron disappeared.

Elizabeth shuddered at the notion that was going through her head. What if Harmon was dangerous enough to have done something to Cameron? What if she was behind Cameron's disappearance? Elizabeth was well aware that Allison was the light of Harmon's life. The more Elizabeth thought about it, the more plausible it seemed that Harmon could be the culprit. Another horrifying idea suddenly formed in Elizabeth's head. What if Peter was in on it? What if the man she had loved and trusted had done something to harm Cameron? The mere thought made her almost physically sick. She needed to accept the fact that Peter being involved with it was a very real possibility at this point. After all, it was obvious that he was in cahoots with Harmon in a major way. It was also obvious to Elizabeth that Harmon had complete control over Peter and had him following her around like a helpless puppy dog who couldn't think for himself.

Elizabeth knew good and well that having a televised commitment ceremony for the entire world to see was Harmon's idea and Harmon's idea alone. Peter may have gone right along with it, but Elizabeth knew that the plan hadn't originated with him. He was just doing everything Harmon told him to do, which caused Elizabeth to wonder just how far Peter's loyalty to Harmon went these days. Was he so completely smitten by her that he would kill his stepdaughter at her instruction? Now, after learning that he ran away with her and that they both disappeared, Elizabeth couldn't help but wonder if he was.

The ringing of Elizabeth's cell phone broke her train of thought.

"Hello," she answered, a little apprehensively since she didn't recognize the number. She hoped someone in the media hadn't somehow got a hold of her cell phone number.

"Am I speaking to Elizabeth Herrington?" a male with a gruff voice asked.

"Yes, this is Elizabeth," she responded nervously.

"Elizabeth, I have your daughter in my possession. If you want to get her back alive, you will do exactly as I say."

Chapter 66

The words spoken by the man on the other end of the phone sent chills down Elizabeth's spine. She had never before heard a voice filled with such meanness and hatred. He was dictating to her what she must do if she wanted to get Cameron back alive. She was listening as best she could, but she was so nervous that she had to keep asking him to repeat himself.

"I'm very sorry," Elizabeth interrupted him again while he was in mid-sentence. "I'm just a little frazzled by everything you're telling me to do. Could you please start over one more time so that I can write it down? I promise this will be the last time. I just want to make sure I know exactly what you want me to do."

Otis was extremely frustrated with her but he knew that if he wanted to accomplish his goal, he was going to have to repeat himself. If he didn't, she wouldn't understand what she was supposed to do.

"Tomorrow night at midnight you will go to the Spanish Steps on Rodeo Drive," Otis said once again. "You will come alone and you will bring ten thousand dollars in cash with you. I will meet you there and will allow you to speak to your daughter via cell phone. That way you will know that she is still alive and well." Otis paused to cough. "You will not get Cameron back tomorrow night, though," he continued.

"The ten thousand dollars is just the first step. I want a lot more than that out of you. I will tell you what I want when I see you tomorrow night. Do you understand everything now? Have I made myself clear?"

Elizabeth's head was spinning as she took it all in.

"Yes," she answered him. "I understand what I'm supposed to do. I do have some questions, though." Otis didn't like the sound of this.

"What do you mean you have questions?" he asked, his overly gruff voice making her feel very nervous. Elizabeth didn't want to scare him off. This was the closest she'd gotten to getting Cameron back so she didn't want to blow it. If Cameron really was alive out there somewhere, she would do absolutely anything to get her released from captivity safely.

"How do I know for sure that you really plan on eventually releasing Cameron to me after I give you the ten thousand dollars? You say that you're not going to release her tomorrow night even after you get the money. How do I know that you will ever follow through with your word?"

Otis began laughing hysterically. It wasn't a nice and jovial laugh, though. It was an evil laugh that made him sound as if he was possessed.

"You really are an interesting woman, Mrs. Herrington," he managed to get out while still laughing. "I was told you were a trip and it turns out I was told correctly. The mere idea of you questioning whether or not I'm going to keep my word is completely absurd. I don't think you quite realize who you're dealing with here. I'm used to getting things done my way without being questioned. If things don't go my way, I become a very dangerous man." He paused to let the words sink in. "I don't think it's very wise of you to question me, Mrs. Herrington, especially since I have your daughter with me. I've killed before and believe me, I'm not afraid to kill again. Please don't make me do something I would rather not be forced to do."

Elizabeth was scared now. She didn't want to do anything to put Cameron's life more at risk than it already was.

"Okay, okay," she said. "I'll take your word that you'll give her back to me eventually. I see that it's the only choice I have in the matter. I'll see you tomorrow night at the Spanish Steps."

Chapter 67

The house on Mulholland Drive was magnificent in every sense of the word. Located halfway between Coldwater Canyon and Laurel Canyon, it offered panoramic views of the San Fernando Valley. Eddie James bought the place ten years ago when he'd first started doing business out here in Los Angeles. An East Coast guy, Eddie enjoyed getting away from New York City every now and then to spend time in the infamous city of Angels.

The house on Mulholland was the hub of Eddie's LA activities… activities which were in no way legal. Eddie was one of the most notorious pimps in the world. His one-of-a-kind prostitution ring had action going on in NYC, LA, Vegas, Miami, and Atlanta. Eddie had luxurious accommodations in all of these cities. He travelled in style, and lived a life of complete and total luxury. The way he saw it, his years of hard work had paid off. Eddie employed some of the hottest girls in the world. He wasn't pimping out trashy girls, His women were top-of-the-line in every way. Most of them were sexy, glamorous, and well-educated.

It was considered an honor to be one of Eddie's working girls. Although it was very difficult to become one, after hired they were some of the highest paid girls in the prostitution industry. Most of them personally banked at least half a million dollars a year. Thanks to Eddie's grooming, they were transformed into real money-making machines. Their clients included some of the world's most rich and famous men; actors, singers, sports superstars, and a lot of wheeler-dealer business types. These individuals were willing to pay top dollar for his services, so Eddie made sure that they always got exactly what they paid for.

One of the main reasons that Eddie's business was so successful was because he had employed excellent people to manage the girls. Each city had a head manager. Under each head manager, there were several other middle managers. The entire reason Eddie was out in LA right now was because his head manager here was in major crisis mode. He wanted to make sure that everything ran smoothly since his manager was currently away and having a lot of very serious personal issues. Eddie sure hoped that Harmon was going to be ok and back to work soon. He really depended on her expertise when it came to running the day-to-day operations.

Chapter 68

Harmon and Peter were enjoying their time on the island more and more every day. It was so nice to not have to worry about the many problems they'd left behind in the states. Now that Harmon was away from Los Angeles, her entire outlook on the situation had changed. She was more at peace with Allison's death than she had been a few weeks ago. She also had a lot less resentment harbored towards Cameron. She still fully believed that Cameron was responsible for her daughter's death, but she wasn't as obsessed with getting revenge as she was before. Having said that, Harmon still wanted for Cameron to have to pay for what she'd done.

She couldn't help but wonder where Cameron had disappeared to. She didn't for a second believe that she'd been kidnapped or committed suicide. Those were two of the popular theories constantly being discussed by the media. Harmon believed that Cameron had run away to avoid being prosecuted for Allison's murder. She believed that Cameron was lying low and hiding out somewhere.

One of the reasons Harmon was mellower now than she was before was because she was madly in love again. She was now fully reunited with the love of her life and she felt both rejuvenated and refreshed. She really felt like everything in her life had finally come full circle. There was still one more thing that needed to be said, though. She wanted to tell Peter the one thing about herself that she'd for so long kept hidden. She wanted to tell him about her job working for Eddie James. She desperately wanted Peter to know about her accomplishments and how successful her career as a madam had been. Even though Harmon knew that career was over, she was still tremendously proud of how good she'd been at executing her job duties. She may have failed in her acting career in her adult years, but her new career had thrived unbelievably. Over the past five years, she'd made over five million dollars. The money didn't come easy, though. She worked extremely hard for such a high pay rate. Harmon essentially ran the prostitution operation out of Eddie's house on Mulholland Drive. She made sure all the girls were well taken care of. The best girls…the one who generated the most revenues, actually got to live in the luxurious house rent-free. Harmon's main job was to basically serve as a mother figure to those girls, many of whom were lost souls. She also oversaw the booking of appointments and all financial transactions. Her job description was definitely wide and varied. Harmon enjoyed being busy, though, so all of the responsibility had given her excellent job satisfaction.

The one thing that Harmon missed the most about LA was her career. Even though she missed it terribly, she knew that she hadn't had any other options but to run away from it all. She was guilty of hiring Leonard Holt to shoot Elizabeth. If she hadn't done the disappearing act, she'd be sitting in a Los Angeles County jail cell right now. Jail was the last place Harmon wanted to be. Even though she had always considered herself to be a tough woman, she didn't think she would be able to handle being incarcerated. She was way too claustrophobic and independent for that. Harmon also knew that she wouldn't be back together with Peter now if they were still in California. It took moving out of state to finally get him away from Elizabeth.

One of the main things that bothered Harmon at this point was that she'd abandoned Eddie James. She'd thought about contacting him to update him on her situation, and to let him know that she wouldn't be returning, but in the end she had decided against that. She just couldn't afford to risk tipping anyone off as to her and Peter's whereabouts. She really did feel bad about it, though, because she and Eddie had enjoyed such a great working relationship with each other over the years. He had trusted her implicitly and she kind of felt that she had betrayed that trust by abandoning him. She really did hope he understood why she'd done what she'd done. Surely he would. Eddie had a lot of really dangerous connections, so she truly hoped he wasn't angry with her. The mere thought of being the object of his wrath completely terrified her. Eddie was a force to be reckoned with.

Chapter 69

It was almost midnight when Eddie James and his entourage of thugs left the house on Mulholland Drive. Altogether, there were six people in the black Suburban that was speeding down Laurel Canyon towards West Hollywood. Eddie, who was sitting in the backseat of the vehicle, was barking out orders. He always sat in the rear seat of the Suburban because the windows were tinted back there, which made him a harder target if someone ever decided to shoot at the vehicle. Eddie James didn't take any chances.

"We can't fuck this up, boys," he yelled. "If we do, we run the risk of losing everything we've worked for. We've got to make sure we get Elizabeth Herrington in this car without any witnesses."

Harvey and Lenny, two of Eddie's main thugs, were visibly nervous about the situation.

"I don't understand why we're meeting her in the middle of Beverly Hills," Harvey growled in a questioning tone. "The Spanish Steps on Rodeo Drive? It just seems too risky."

Lenny nodded his head in agreement. Eddie couldn't have been anymore irritated with them. They acted like this on every job he gave them these days. It was like they were getting soft or something, and it irritated the hell out of him. If they weren't so damn good at what they did, he'd get rid of them.

"I just don't know about this boss," Harvey continued. "Seems like we're asking for trouble going about it this way."

Eddie let out a huge groan as the Suburban turned right off Laurel Canyon onto Sunset.

"Will you please just shut the fuck up!?" he yelled. "You're both acting like imbeciles. Nothing is going to go wrong. We're meeting her on Rodeo Drive because I know she'll feel safer there. I'm trying to get her to let her guard down." As he explained himself, Harvey, Lenny, and everyone else in the car began to feel a little more confident about things. They were now speeding down the Sunset Strip. Traffic was light this late. It was quickly approaching midnight. The driver of the vehicle took a left on Doheny and then a right onto Santa Monica Boulevard. They were now in Beverly Hills and only a few blocks away from Rodeo Drive. Eddie took out his phone and called Elizabeth.

"Hello," she answered on the first ring. She sounded nervous.

"Hi there," Eddie said, his voice icy. "We're almost there. Are you waiting for us?"

Chapter 70

Elizabeth was sitting on the Spanish Steps, completely scared out of her mind. The Beverly Wilshire Hotel, which was directly across the street, towered above her. She was talking on her cell phone.

"Yeah, I'm here waiting on you," she said, her fear evident by the trembling of her voice.

"Are you alone?" the strange male voice asked.

"Yes, I came alone," Elizabeth lied, hoping the caller didn't already know that John was sitting in his car on Wilshire about a block away from the hotel. John had come to watch her to make sure she was safe and that nothing bad happened. Elizabeth gasped as a black Suburban suddenly turned off of Rodeo onto Wilshire and stopped directly in front of her. She tried to screams as two huge men jumped out of the vehicle and ran towards her. Her cries were muffled as they threw her into the back of the Suburban and gagged and bound her.

The vehicle was now speeding back the same route it had come. Elizabeth was completely panicked now. A million thoughts were racing through her head, and not one of them was reassuring or comforting. She now realized that she'd made a huge mistake by not getting the police involved in this situation. She could only hope that John was following in his car.

"It's good to meet you, Elizabeth" the man sitting next to her in the backseat suddenly said. She was blindfolded, so she couldn't see what he looked like. She recognized his voice, though. It was the man she'd been talking to on the phone.

"I'm Eddie James," he said. "Please don't hyperventilate. We're taking you to your daughter now."

Elizabeth couldn't help but notice how strangely calm this Eddie guy's voice was. He seemed to be totally cool and collected, even in this unbelievably stressful situation. Although she was blindfolded and couldn't see, she was fairly certain that they were now somewhere in the hills. The car was slowly climbing upwards.

Elizabeth had never felt this scared before. She didn't know what was going to happen to her. She'd been kidnapped by these men, and had no idea what they planned to do to her. The man had said he wasn't going to harm her, but Elizabeth didn't put any confidence in his words. He was obviously a psychotic maniac. Elizabeth now knew how her daughter must have felt when she was kidnapped. It must have been absolutely terrifying for her.

Chapter 71

It was pouring down rain on the island. Peter and Harmon were sitting in the living room of Bob's mansion. Peter couldn't believe what he was hearing. His wife, the love his life, was a madam. It seemed implausible to him that Harmon Herrington, who was Hollywood royalty, had stooped so low. As he sat here listening to her try to explain herself, he became even more disgusted. She kept bragging about how much money she'd made off of it. He didn't give a damn how much money she'd made. She was already rich and didn't need the money. The whole thing completely repulsed him.

"I can't believe you did this," Peter said, not trying to hide his disappointment. "I thought you were more respectable than that."

Harmon was devastated by Peter's reaction. She had wanted him to be proud of her for her great achievements, but instead he was ashamed of her. Instead of being angry by his reaction, Harmon was crushed. Her entire self-esteem was crumbling right before her. She desperately wanted Peter's seal of approval. She suddenly started crying. Harmon felt like a little girl as she stared into her husband's disapproving face.

"I wanted to be successful at something," Harmon sobbed. "When my acting career fizzled and I stopped getting parts, I felt like such a failure. Finding this new career revitalized me and made me feel whole again," she said.

Even though Peter was furious with her, he couldn't help but feel sorry for her. As he looked into her eyes, he could see how frail her mental state was right now. She truly was in a very bad place. He reached over to hug her and decided to quit being so hard on her.

"I definitely don't agree with what you did," he said. "I know that you're a very smart woman and you could've used your smarts for so much more," he continued. "Prostitution is just so dirty and low-class." As he said these things, Harmon began to feel ashamed. She wasn't ashamed because she felt like she'd done anything wrong, though. She was ashamed because she knew how badly she had disappointed Peter. She was now crying with her face buried in his chest. She could hardly bear to look at him. Harmon didn't regret her career with Eddie. She only regretted telling Peter. She wished she could turn the clocks back an hour and not make the confession to him. Harmon knew she couldn't turn the clocks back, though. There was no way to reverse time and save face. She was going to have to make the best of things and go forward. It wasn't like Peter's disapproval was the end of the world. From the way he was talking, he wasn't going to leave her. He just wasn't going to applaud her career choices.

"I don't want you to ever work in that field again," Peter said. "And you need to stay away from this Eddie James guy. He sounds like bad news."

Harmon looked directly into Peter's eyes.

"I'm truly sorry," she lied. "If I had known how negatively you feel about prostitution, I never would have become involved with it."

Peter could tell she was lying, but he didn't really care. They weren't ever going back to LA again anyway, so it didn't matter if Harmon repented. Her career as a madam and her working relationship with Eddie James were both history at this point. Peter was glad that at least he knew to watch Harmon like a hawk now. He needed to make sure that she never became involved with such craziness again.

Peter knew that he would have more questions for Harmon later about her past. All he wanted to do right now was change the subject and not dwell on anything negative.

"I sure do love this island," he said awkwardly, not knowing how to gradually change the subject.

"I love it too," Harmon said with a half-smile. She wiped the tears from her eyes. "It's beautiful. I can't think of any other place I'd rather be right now."

"I wonder if we'll live here forever or only temporarily," Peter said, thinking aloud. He felt that they would have to go somewhere else eventually. He just wasn't sure when that would be. The island was absolutely perfect for now, though.

The rain was still coming down in torrents when the phone rang. Both Peter and Harmon jumped a little when they heard the ring. Peter looked at the caller ID and saw that it was Marlin, his friend and the owner of the island.

"Hey Marlin," he answered after the second ring. "What's up?"

"Hey," Marlin said. "How are you and Harmon?" Peter could tell by the tone of Marlin's voice that something was terribly wrong.

"Harmon and I are fine," he said hurriedly. "What's wrong? What's going on?"

"Look Peter," his friend said. "I know we've been friends for a long time, but I didn't quite realize what I was getting myself into when I agreed to let you and Harmon hide out on the island." Marlin paused for a moment, and Peter could feel himself beginning to panic. "I know I've been involved in some shady stuff over the years," Marlin continued. "But all my businesses have been clean for years now. If I continue to harbor Harmon, I'm going to wind up in prison myself. She's a fugitive."

"So what are you trying to tell me, Marlin?" Peter interrupted.

Marlin hesitated for a moment and then continued.

"I'm telling you that I called the authorities a little while ago and told them where you and Harmon are."

Chapter 72

They were now at the house on Mulholland Drive. Elizabeth was un-blindfolded and led into the house by Eddie and his entourage of thugs. She was surprised at the opulence of her surroundings. The place was immaculate and furnished with the finest European antiques. She'd really never seen anything quite like it. That was really saying something since she'd lived in Beverly Hills for several years now. The rough-looking men in the house definitely didn't fit the furnishings, though. She'd never been around men so scary, gross, and overbearing. The language coming out of their mouths was complete and total filth. Elizabeth was so scared because she had no idea what to expect next. She didn't know what these men were going to do to her.

She became even more scared as they led her down a flight of stairs to the basement. The basement, which was very dark and lit by a few dim lights, was crammed full of junk. Everything down there appeared to be at least 30 years old. Elizabeth thought it looked almost like a museum because there was so much stuff there. At the back of the basement there was another small door. The men led Elizabeth through the door and down another spiral staircase that took them even further below ground. She was a little disoriented, but it appeared that they were now walking down a tunnel far below the house. The tunnel, which was very dark and winding, seemed like it went on forever. The only thing lighting their way was a flashlight that one of the men brought with them.

They finally reached the end of the passageway and Elizabeth let out screams of both horror and joy at what she saw. Cameron was lying on a cot in a small cell. Bars covered the cell just like a real jail cell. Both Elizabeth and Cameron started crying once they saw each other. The men yelled for them to shut up as they opened the cell door and made Elizabeth go inside. Now that they were both locked up, they embraced and were crying hysterically. Elizabeth was too overjoyed at seeing her daughter alive to think about the fact that she had now been kidnapped too. Neither one of them noticed as the men left the cell and made their way back up the passageway.

"I can't believe you're ok," Elizabeth sobbed, holding on to her daughter as tightly as she could. "I've been so worried about you. We thought you may be dead. We had no idea what could have happened…" Elizabeth was rambling almost incoherently because she was so flustered that she and Cameron had been reunited. It truly was like a dream come true, despite the dismal circumstances. She was just now beginning to realize that she was a prisoner now too.

"This place is really cold," Elizabeth said with a shiver, folding her arms together.

"You get used to it," Cameron said. Her hair was oily from not washing it regularly and her face was all broken out with acne because she wasn't able to maintain herself down here.

"Who are these people?" Elizabeth asked. "Why did they kidnap you?"

"The guy who's in charge is named Eddie James," Cameron said. She had learned a lot about this place the last few weeks. "He runs some sort of prostitution ring, and Allison apparently worked for him as a call girl. He had her killed because she wanted to stop working for him. From what they told me, she rebelled against him and wanted to live a normal life, so he'd had her killed because she knew too much. He then had me kidnapped because he was afraid that Allison may have confided the truth to me before she was killed."

Elizabeth was completely flabbergasted at what she was hearing. The story was so crazy, she felt like the whole world was spinning out of control. She literally felt dizzy as she tried to digest the news. She knew that Allison was a little on the wild side at times, but she would have never guessed that she was involved with prostitution. She had had everything going for her, and she definitely didn't need the money. It made no sense to her why a girl like Allison would become involved with something like that.

"You want to know the worst part?" Cameron said, giving Elizabeth a disgusted look.

"What?" she asked.

"Harmon was her madam. She works for Eddie James too."

Chapter 73

Peter was going completely crazy. He was running all over the house yelling and screaming. Harmon was chasing after him, begging him to calm down and hold himself together. She was panicked too, but she wanted to think about the situation calmly and come up with a reasonable solution. Behaving like this wasn't going to solve anything. The rain was still poring torrentially outside. The entire house was shaking from the intensity of the roaring thunder of the storm.

"I can't believe that son of a bitch sold us out," Peter yelled for the third time. "That low-life scum of the earth son of a bitch." He was so enraged he was foaming at the mouth. Harmon couldn't help but be a little scared that he was about to have a heart attack. She had never seen anyone this upset before.

"I know what we have to do," Peter said, still in hysterics. "We have to end this together. It's the only way. We don't have enough time to escape. The police will be here any minute."

"What are you talking about?" Harmon asked, not understanding what Peter was saying. "End what?"

Peter grabbed onto her and held her close. He lowered his voice and looked directly into her eyes.

"It's the only way, Harmon," he said. "We have to make a suicide pact and end our lives right now if you want to escape going to prison. That's the only way we're going to be together forever. It's our only chance at true love."

Harmon couldn't believe what she was hearing. It sounded crazy, but she knew he was speaking the truth. It was like this was all pre-destined or something…the way the gods wanted it. What Peter was saying actually made perfect sense. Ending their lives together now seemed to be the only way they were going to be happy. Harmon still had doubts, though, even though she was slowly accepting the truth.

"Are you sure about this? She asked him, looking deep into his eyes. "Is this really the right thing to do?"

All of a sudden they started kissing each other slowly. The kisses were deep and passionate. Harmon felt truly safe, secure, and at peace for the first time in a very long time. Everything felt right for both of them.

"I'm positive," Peter said, pulling away from his wife gently. "The authorities are out to get us. Everyone is against us. It's you and me against the whole world, baby. It's time to throw in the towel and just give the middle finger to this whole fucked up planet."

Harmon felt a rush of excitement as she thought about it. This was her chance to escape all the pain she felt…the pain of losing her daughter. She had just now begun to accept the fact that Eddie James was most likely behind Allison's death since Allison had pissed him off by not wanting to work for him anymore. Until this point, Harmon hadn't wanted to admit the truth to herself. She felt too guilty about everything. Deep down, though, she knew that Allison was dead because of her. If she hadn't become involved with Eddie James, then Allison wouldn't have either. Allison only knew Eddie through her. She'd introduced Allison to him because she'd wanted to give her daughter the opportunity to make a lot of money. Harmon now realized that by doing so she had essentially sold her daughter's soul to the devil. As she thought about it, she burst into tears.

Peter didn't know exactly why Harmon was crying, but he could tell by looking in her eyes that she agreed with him and had accepted their destiny of death. It was at that exact moment that both Peter and Harmon heard the helicopters churning overhead. The authorities were here.

"Come on," Peter said, grabbing Harmon's hand and running out the front door of the house. "We have to hurry if we're going to do this properly."

Peter and Harmon ran from the house and into the nearby woods. Peter was leading the way on the trail that led to the cliff. The rain was still coming down in torrents. They were now on the other side of the wooded area, still running. Harmon was completely out of breath and begging Peter to slow down. Peter continued running, though, pulling his wife behind him. They were splashing through mud puddle after mud puddle. Several helicopters were circling overhead with their lights shining down on the island.

Peter and Harmon were now at the cliff. As they stood hand in hand, they looked down at the water more than 200 feet below them. The authorities in the helicopters had now spotted them and were shining the searchlights directly on them. The rain was now coming down even harder. The two of them were completely drenched. To make matters worse, the authorities in the helicopters were now barking out orders over a loudspeaker.

"Put your hands in the air," the voice yelled.

The scene was complete and total chaos. Peter and Harmon were making out in the middle of it all, proving to everyone that they both really were nuts.

"I love you, Harmon," Peter said to his soul mate as he stared into her beautiful brown eyes.

"I love you too," Harmon responded, clasping her husband's hand. "You're the only person in the world who ever truly meant anything to me." Peter and Harmon were both crying now. Neither one of them had ever felt so emotional.

"Remember when we first met, I told you we'd be together forever?" Peter suddenly asked, wiping the tears from his eyes.

Harmon nodded her head.

"Yes," she said with a faint smile. "We both knew we were ride or die from the very beginning."

"Now it's time to begin our new journey," Peter whispered into her ear, brushing her cheek. "It's time for us to become angels."

With that, they both closed their eyes and jumped from the cliff. As the shallow water and jagged rocks rushed up to greet them, they were both screaming in terror. The scene was complete and total chaos. Peter and Harmon quickly met their destinies…two of the most tragic deaths to ever occur…forever together…forever crazy.

Chapter 74

The scene at the house on Mulholland Drive was just as crazy as the events taking place on the island. As the police raided the hillside home of Eddie James, they were sprayed with bullets coming from the machine guns of Eddie's thugs. Eddie himself was running around the place with his Uzi firing randomly. He was in total shock at what was taking place. They'd been completely ambushed and caught off guard. Several officers lost their lives, but Eddie's associates were eventually all handcuffed and arrested. Eddie himself was found in the backyard hiding in a tree.

The police had raided the place once John called them and told them that Elizabeth had been kidnapped. He was able to give them the address because he'd followed Eddie's Suburban from Rodeo Drive after they'd taken Elizabeth against her will. John was standing out front when Eddie James was taken out of the home in handcuffs.

"You little bastard," Eddie yelled at him. "You think you're so fucking smart don't you." Even though it was dark outside, John could tell that Eddie's face was red with rage. He also recognized the voice. Eddie was the anonymous caller and the killer of his first wife and two daughters

"Why did you do it?" John yelled at him. "Why did you kill Kelly, Molly, and Grace?"

"Because your wife was nothing but a whore," Eddie spat. "She was a madam just like Harmon. She wanted out of the lifestyle, though, so I had to axe her because she knew too much. That's what happened to Allison too. She knew too much for her own damn good."

John didn't say a word back to Eddie. He just stared at him in shock. This was really the first time that he'd felt as if he was staring true evil directly in the face. After a few short moments, John turned to the police officer standing beside him.

"Are Elizabeth and Cameron ok?" he asked.

"Yeah, we found them in an old cell way underneath the house. There's a secret tunnel that leads to where they were. One of Eddie's guys caved in and showed it to us once we started questioning him. The guy also told us that Eddie kidnapped Elizabeth because he'd wanted to take her away from you. Apparently, Eddie has a really big grudge against you because you were acquitted of the crime he committed against your wife and daughters. He wanted you to go down for the crime so that no one would ever suspect him. Once you were acquitted, he made it part of his life mission to torture you to get back at you."

John just shook his head in disbelief. He didn't even say anything because it was all too crazy to even process. This whole thing really was so far beyond logical. John had never felt so disgusted in his life.

Epilogue

After Peter and Harmon's bodies were recovered from the ocean, Steven had the authorities ship them back to the States, where he gave them a proper burial. The funeral he had for them was small and attended only by close family friends. The people closest to him that was present were John, Elizabeth, and Cameron. These three came more out of respect for Steven than because of any loyalty they felt towards Harmon and Peter. Elizabeth did sob throughout the ceremony, though, because she was so conflicted about the feelings she felt towards her now late-husband. What saddened her most was that her son would grow up without knowing his father.

Although the funeral itself was small and low-key, the media frenzy outside the church was another story altogether. It seemed like every paparazzo in LA was gathered together there trying to catch a glimpse of the attendees. While it was true that Peter and Harmon had hurt a lot of people, it was very important to Steven to give them a nice funeral. He even had them buried in Forest Lawn Memorial Park so that they would be close by. He wanted to feel that they were close to him in the days to come, which wouldn't be easy, considering he was now the only member of his family alive.

Steven had experienced so much loss this past year. He'd lost his sister and now both of his parents. He knew he was going to be ok, though. He had a great support system. These past few weeks, he'd become so close to Elizabeth, John, and now Cameron. He knew they genuinely cared for him and would be in his life forever. He might not have his blood family anymore, but he did have his stepmother and stepsister, and that he was truly grateful for.

After the funeral, Steven enrolled at USC, where he decided to pursue a degree in general business. He still wanted to own a bar one day, but he knew he needed a solid business background in order to successfully operate the high-class establishment he hoped to open. It made him really happy to know how proud his mom and dad would be to know that he'd finally gone back to school and established a true sense of direction for his future. He actually had goals now, and he was determined to not stop until he achieved them. He knew it wasn't going to be an easy road, but nothing worth achieving ever was easy.

Steven moved out of the Malibu beach house and got a small apartment close to campus. One thing he was really excited about was starting to date again. Now that he'd grown up and matured, he had changed his whole dating strategy. This time around he was looking for a girl he could have a real and meaningful relationship with. He was no longer the Steven Herrington he used to be…the guy who viewed life as one continuous party and who objectified women. These days he was ambitious and respectable, and everyone he knew couldn't be any more proud of him.

* * *

The prostitution empire run by Eddie James completely crumbled after the shootout at the house on Mulholland. Eddie was charged with hiring someone to murder Allison Herrington. He also faced numerous other charges, including the kidnapping of Cameron. His trial, which took place in Los Angeles, was an international news sensation. He was sentenced to life in prison without parole, and Elizabeth and John couldn't have been anymore thrilled. They hoped he never saw the light of day again after everything he'd done to them.

The employees of Eddie James were quickly arrested in cities all around the country. Many of them also got very strict sentences for their involvement. Even after his trial ended, Eddie still couldn't believe how quickly everything fell apart for him. He'd been so successful at his business just to have everything taken away from him like this. It was definitely a humbling experience, and he couldn't help but be very bitter about the way things had turned out. Eddie also confessed to hiring someone to murder Joey from Joey's Bar.

"His niece, Samantha Taylor, was another one of the girls I had working for me. She was one of my best hookers, but like Allison, she wanted out of the business. Joey was helping her try to get out, so Joey had to go."

Samantha never showed up. No one knew exactly where she was or what happened to her, but they all genuinely hoped she was at peace and living a happy life wherever she was.

* * *

After the truth regarding the Herrington case came out, Carter Greenfield fled to Europe, just like he said he would. It didn't seem like Carter was ever going to change, as Cameron and Steven heard through friends that he was on a never-ending drug-binge and constantly in the hospital for overdosing. Although it saddened Cameron to know that the father of her child was so lost in the world, she knew it was for the best that he didn't play a part in the kid's life right now. She didn't want to expose the baby to such an unhealthy situation. Cameron prayed every day that Carter would change one day, though. She dreamed of the day where he could meet his son, who she'd named after him. Carter Jr. was a vivacious and extremely happy little boy. Steven was named the baby's godfather, as he was Cameron's stepbrother and the best friend of the older Carter.

* * *

Cameron continued to live with Carter Jr. and Elizabeth in the Herrington mansion in Beverly Hills. They'd thought about moving and buying a new home, but Elizabeth wanted her son and grandson to grow up in the family home. The home had so much history to it, and despite all the bad that had happened there, a feeling of love permeated the residence. The knowledge that Allison had died in the upstairs bathroom didn't creep them out. It actually made them feel closer to her than ever before.

Cameron had a hard time coming to terms with the fact that Allison had been a high-class prostitute. It made her feel better to know that Allison hadn't liked the lifestyle and had wanted to get out, though. It completely disgusted her that Eddie had had her murdered just because he'd been afraid that she would go to the authorities and expose his illegal escort service if he wouldn't allow her to quit working for him. He'd wanted her to be a slave for him, and he'd taken matters into his own hands when she'd tried to free herself from a terrible situation.

Like Steven, Cameron also enrolled in classes. She registered at Valley College, and only went to school two days a week. She wasn't entirely sure what she wanted to do with the rest of her life career-wise, but she knew she had a while to figure it out. The one thing she did know for sure, though, was that she wanted to be the best mother she could possibly be. She wanted to spend the right amount of time nurturing Carter Jr. so that he would know that he was wanted and a huge blessing in his family's life.

* * *

Winston Herrington was born just a few weeks after his father, Peter's death. John and Cameron were both in the room with Elizabeth when he made his grand arrival. Carter Jr. was born just a few days before. Winston was a beautiful baby and looked so much like his mother. Elizabeth couldn't believe how lucky she was to have a baby this late in life. She felt that Winston brought fresh and new energy into her existence, which is exactly what she needed after all the bad that had happened this past year. The baby truly was a blessing that she knew she would never take for granted. Elizabeth also thanked God every day that her beautiful daughter, Cameron, was found alive and well after being locked in a desolate cell for so many weeks. In a way, she felt as if she was getting a second chance now, so she was determined to make sure her future was bright. In order to do that, she had to become financially stable on her own now that she didn't have the Herrington money to help her out.

Not long after Winston's birth, Elizabeth got her real estate license and quickly became the premier real estate agent to the stars. She was able to use her notoriety to her advantage, and make some serious money selling some of the largest homes in Los Angeles. Everyone who was anyone called her when they wanted to buy or sell property in the area. Once she became super successful, John Parker followed in her footsteps and got his real estate license as well. He wanted to have a stable job that he enjoyed since his screenwriting career hadn't panned out yet. Because of this, John went to work at the real estate agency that Elizabeth had opened up.

A few months after Allison's murder case was solved, John set to work on writing a screenplay based off the events. It was still too soon to tell, but everyone who he'd discussed the idea with thought it was very promising that a major studio would pick up the project. It seemed as if the entire world was still completely fascinated with the Herrington family saga.

* * *

John Parker finally felt both happy and free. For the first time since the death of his wife and daughters, he wasn't looking over his shoulder expecting someone to find out who he was. Throughout the trial, John had been terrified that the media would find out he was Neil Hudson. Although the police knew the truth, the media hadn't made the connection. At this point, he didn't even care if they did find out. He was now comfortable in his own skin and totally at peace since he knew who was behind the murder of his family. He still couldn't believe that their deaths were connected to Eddie James' prostitution ring.

It seemed so completely insane to learn that his wife, Kelly, had been the madam for the city of Atlanta at the time of her death. John had always wondered how she made so much money at her real estate job, but it turns out real estate wasn't all she was involved in. Eddie had confessed that Kelly had wanted to make a change and leave the business, so he'd hired someone to kill her because she knew too much. He'd then taken a serious dislike to John, who had still been Neil Hudson at the time, because he was acquitted for the murders of Kelly and the girls. Eddie had wanted for John to go down for the crimes so that no one would ever investigate the situation more closely and find out the truth. Eddie confessed to the police that he had devised the most ingenious plan to get back at John once he found him in LA after looking for him for close to five years. He'd paid Harmon to start a relationship with him so that he could start to torture him by calling him and playing cruel mind games. The ultimate plan had been to murder John just like he'd had his family murdered back in Atlanta. The full truth about what all had happened made John's head spin. It was almost too much to take in. Although he hadn't loved Harmon for that long, he was still disappointed that she'd essentially started a fake relationship with him just to screw with him. John refused to believe that the entire relationship had been fake, though. He knew that couldn't be true because Harmon had really seemed to love him. It may have started out with her being paid by Eddie James to pursue him, but she'd fallen for him. That he was certain of. Despite the disturbing details, John was at peace with both Harmon's death and his memories of their rocky relationship. Even after all she'd done wrong in her life, he refused to believe that she was an evil person. She was just a misguided, insecure, and conflicted woman who had never been content with herself. She'd spent her life chasing dreams that were unattainable, and trying to be something she wasn't.

Even though John was terribly disappointed that his late wife, Kelly, had been instrumental in such a disgusting business, he was so grateful that after all these years he knew the truth. There were no unanswered questions now. He could truly close the door on his past and move forward with his new life here in Los Angeles. He was almost certain that his new life involved Elizabeth Herrington, and not just as his real estate partner. He cared a lot about her, and was feeling all kinds of feelings he hadn't felt in years.

* * *

A few months after Peter and Harmon's funeral, John finally got the courage to ask Elizabeth on an official date. The two of them went to Geoffrey's in Malibu, where they were seated on a patio overlooking the Pacific Ocean. The setting couldn't have been any more beautiful. John looked magnificent in his Armani suit, and Elizabeth looked more fabulous than ever in her Chanel gown. Together they ate and watched the beautiful sunset. They weren't exactly a couple yet, but John was certain that they would be eventually. The mere thought made him feel warm with joy and excitement. It was at that moment that he knew his future was going to be better than he'd ever dreamed.

About the Author

Roman St. John is a writer of mystery and suspense novels. His first book, *Buried Secrets*, was released under the name Jonathan Ross. *Hollywood Malice* is his second novel. St. John lives in Los Angeles.

CPSIA information can be obtained at www.ICGtesting.com
Printed in the USA
LVOW06s0422140414

381579LV00013B/387/P